Fink's Funk

Cover illustration by Serge Bloch

Book design by Janet Kusmierski

ISBN 0-439-57472-2

12 11 10 9 8 7 6 5 4 3 2 1   4 5 6 7 8 9/0

Printed in the U.S.A.   40
First printing, December 2004

Boyds will Be Boyds™

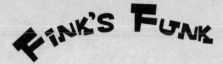

Fink's Funk

by sarah weeks

AN
APPLE
PAPERBACK

SCHOLASTIC INC.

New York Toronto London Auckland Sydney
Mexico City New Delhi Hong Kong Buenos Aires

For Audrey, my very first best friend—S.W.

CHAPTER ONE

*

I'm crazy about Tallulah. The minute I laid eyes on her, I knew she was the one for me. She has the sweetest face in the world, the most beautiful, intelligent eyes, and you wouldn't believe how soft and pink her skin is.

Wait! Slow down! Before you get any weird ideas about me liking girls, let me make it perfectly clear that Tallulah is not a girl. She's a rat. A hairless rat, to be exact. And she's the best rat in the whole world.

"Hey, Fink, you gotta see this! Get over here as soon as you can, okay?"

I hung up the phone, pulled up my sleeve, and looked at my watch. Fink's record time, running from his house to mine, was fifty-seven seconds. Would he beat it?

Less than a minute later, Fink flung open the door of my room and fell on the floor, panting.

"How did I do?" he gasped.

"Fifty-eight seconds," I said.

"Close," he said.

"Yeah, but you know what they say — Close only counts in horseshoes."

Fink didn't bother to ask me where I'd picked that up. He knows one of my mom's expressions when he hears one. He got up, brushed himself off, and sat on the edge of my bed.

"Are you sure you timed that right?" he asked. "It felt like I was moving faster than ever. I even jumped over that big bush next to your porch so I could save time by not having to run up the steps."

"Nope, sorry. It was fifty-eight seconds on the dot," I said.

"The problem is that I didn't have my usual bowl of Crackle Puffs this morning," said Fink, still trying to catch his breath. "We were all out, so my mom made me scrambled eggs instead. That must be what slowed me down."

"I can't believe your mom lets you eat Crackle Puffs for breakfast. They're pure sugar, you know," I said.

"I know. Why do you think I love them so much?" asked Fink. "So, what's so important that I had to break the sound barrier getting over here?"

"Talullah's got a new trick," I said.

"Really? Another one? How many does that make so far?"

"Three."

"I remember the cheese cup, but what else does she do?" asked Fink.

The cheese cup was the very first trick I taught Tallulah. The way it works is, I take two little paper cups — the kind you use for mouthwash — and put a chunk of cheddar cheese under one of them. Tallulah sniffs the cups and then knocks over the one with the cheese under it. She gets it right every time.

"She dances," I said, "remember?"

"Oh, yeah! I love that trick," said Fink. "It's so funny."

Technically, she doesn't actually "dance." I make a kissing sound and she stands up on her hind legs and tries to keep her balance while she waits for me to give her the snack she knows I'm going to give her every time she hears the kissing sound. But Fink and I both like to call it dancing since Tallulah was named after Tallulah Treehaven, this nutty dancer with gigantic false eyelashes, who came to our class earlier in the year to do a project with us.

"Okay, are you ready for the new trick?" I asked, reaching into the glass tank and gently picking up Tallulah.

"Ready," said Fink.

I held a piece of cheese in front of Tallulah's nose so she could get a good whiff of it. Then I put it in my shirt pocket. "Get the cheese, Tallulah!" I said as I stretched open the cuff at the end of my shirt.

Tallulah knew what to do. She ran right up my arm! You could see the bulge as she made her way up my arm, over my shoulder, and then out between the top two buttons of my shirt. Her whiskers danced as she picked up the scent of the cheese and dove quickly into my pocket to retrieve it.

"Cool!" said Fink. "Can I try?"

"Sure, but I should warn you, it tickles," I told him.

We took turns letting Tallulah run up our arms, until she'd had so much cheese, she lost interest in the game. I put her back in her cage, a glass tank with a screen lid, and after a short run in her exercise wheel, she crawled under the pile of cotton balls she'd made into a fluffy nest, and went to sleep.

"Isn't she the best?" I asked.

"Yeah," said Fink. "And I never thought I'd say this, but I don't even mind that she's bald anymore."

We left Tallulah sleeping, and went downstairs to have a snack.

"You want to eat up in the tree?" I asked.

"Sure," said Fink.

Fink and I have a favorite spot to hang out, high in the branches of a big old tree in my backyard. Actually, it's not quite as high as we used to think it was when we were younger (and shorter).

"What are you going to teach Tallulah next?" Fink asked once we'd settled in the tree with a bag of pretzels to munch on.

"I'm not sure," I said. "Got any ideas?"

That was a silly question. Fink *always* has ideas. They're not always *good* ideas, but he has an endless supply of them.

"Remember in that book, *Charlotte's Web*, how Charlotte the spider wove words into her web? Maybe you should try to teach Tallulah how to do something like that," suggested Fink.

"Weave a web, you mean?" I asked.

"No, *read*."

"That was a made-up story, Fink. Real spiders can't read and write," I said. "But wait a second, wasn't there a rat in that story, too?"

"Yeah, he was the one who got the words for Charlotte out of old newspapers."

"But he couldn't read the words himself, remember?" I said. "Even fictional rats can't read."

"Tallulah is much smarter than that rat was," said Fink. "How do you know she can't read?"

"I don't know for sure, but let's just say I have a hunch."

"If George Washington Carver had had a hunch that peanuts wouldn't taste good if you mashed them up and spread them on bread, he might never have invented peanut butter," Fink said. "Did you ever think of that?"

I am very happy to report I had NOT ever thought of that. One person in the world who thinks like Fink is plenty.

"I wish *we* could invent something," said Fink. "Wouldn't it be great if a hundred years from now, two kids were sitting up in a tree talking about something we'd thought up?"

"We've invented stuff," I said.

"We have?"

"Sure. We've invented lots of games, haven't we?" I asked.

"Oh, that reminds me, Nat-man. I've been meaning to tell you I've decided you're right about the Rhyming Game. It is getting kind of boring. We need to come up with something new."

"Necessity is the mother of invention," I told him.

"Let's invent a new game right now," said Fink, grabbing a handful of pretzels and shoving a bunch in his mouth. "Hah-wah-boff-agawm —" Not only was Fink spraying crumbs all over the place but he was also making it impossible to tell what he was saying.

"Say it, don't spray it," I told him.

Fink finished chewing, swallowed the pretzels, and wiped his mouth on his sleeve.

"Sorry about that," he said. "What I was trying to say was, how about a game where we have to decide what the funniest word is?"

"I don't get it. Give me an example."

"Okay, which word is funnier, *yodel* or *peanut*?" he asked.

"Um . . . neither one of them is particularly funny, but if I had to choose one, I guess I'd say *yodel* is funnier," I answered.

"Good. Now which is funnier, *yodel* or *poodle*?"

"I don't know. It's a tie," I said.

"How about *poodle* or *puddle*?" asked Fink.

"This game is even worse than the Rhyming Game," I said.

Fink told me if I was going to be picky about it, I should go ahead and try to think of something better myself. I thought about it for a minute.

"Okay, how about this — every day, each of us has to come up with an interesting fact. Whoever's fact is the most interesting wins for that day."

Fink smiled.

"I like it! But what do we do if I think my fact is more interesting than yours, and you think yours is more interesting than mine?" he asked. "How do we decide who wins?"

"Good question. Maybe we should let somebody else decide."

"Who?" Fink asked.

"It would have to be somebody smart enough to recognize a good fact when they hear one," I said.

"How about my mom?" asked Fink. "She's pretty smart. She does the whole Sunday crossword puzzle in pen and she's got a Ph.D. I'm sure she'd be willing to be a judge for us."

"No way! She can't be our judge, Fink. She'd be totally biased. You're her precious little Boydey-boy. She had coffee mugs made with your face printed on them, remember? You think she'd ever vote against you?"

"She hardly ever uses those mugs anymore," said Fink, blushing a little.

"Still," I said, "moms are totally out."

"So, who are we going to get to be the judge?" he asked. Then a slow sly smile spread across his face. "I know, how about your girlfriend?"

"I don't have a girlfriend, and you know it!" I shouted.

"I hate to break it to you, Nat-o, but *she* thinks you do."

He was talking about Leslie Zebak. At first, she'd had a thing for Fink, but ever since I'd borrowed some pet supplies for Tallulah from her, unfortunately she'd had a major crush on me instead.

"I got another note from her yesterday," I told him. "She put so much perfume on it, I got a headache."

"Ugh! I remember when I was the one she used to send those stinky love notes to," Fink said with a shudder. "I'm so glad she's moved on to you."

"Gee, thanks a lot," I said. "What a pal."

"You know, now that I'm thinking about it, it probably wouldn't be such a good idea to ask Leslie to be the judge, either," said Fink.

"Why not?"

"If you think my mom would be biased, believe me, Leslie would be even worse. She's crazy about you," said Fink.

"*Crazy* is the right word for it," I said. "Last week she picked all the lint balls off my sweater while she was sitting behind me at assembly. I thought she was just doing me a favor, but it turns out she kept them and put them in a locket that she wears on a chain around her neck now. How sick is that?"

"Next thing you know, she'll be having coffee mugs made with your face on them," said Fink.

"She scares me," I said with a shudder. "So, who are we going to get to be our judge?"

"What we need is someone really smart who doesn't like either one of us very much," Fink said.

We looked at each other. Of course! It was so obvious!

"Corn Bloomers!" we both said at the exact same time.

CHAPTER TWO

*

"Jinx on Froozles!" I shouted as I punched Fink in the arm so hard he lost his balance and almost fell out of the tree.

"Whoa!" he said, grabbing on to a branch to steady himself. "Take it easy, will you, Nat-o?"

"Sorry, Fink. I didn't mean to hit you that hard. It's just that I've had a lot more practice being punched than doing the punching. As you've probably noticed, you usually beat me at this game."

I'm not sure why people say "jinx" on stuff when they say the same thing at the same time by accident, but they do. And with Fink and me, it's always been "Jinx on Froozles." Froozles, in case you don't know,

13

are giant milk shakes they sell down at the Bee Hive snack bar.

"Corn Bloomers would make the perfect judge," Fink said, rubbing the sore spot on his arm where I had just punched him.

"Yeah. Jessie loves to tell people what she thinks," I said. "Plus, don't tell her I said so, but she's pretty smart."

"Not as smart as she thinks she is, though," said Fink.

"Definitely not. But I think she's smart enough to do this job. And most important, she doesn't like either one of us."

"Right," said Fink. "She'll make a perfect judge."

"But what about Marla?" I asked.

"What about her? Don't tell me you think she'd make a better judge than Jessie Kornblume? She's half as smart and twice as annoying."

He was right about that, but I wasn't suggesting that I wanted Marla to be our judge. All I was saying is that she might *have* to be a judge.

"Why?" asked Fink.

14

"Because, you know how it works, Finker. The Red Devils do everything together," I said.

"Oh, I see what you're saying. Jessie won't do it unless Marla does it, too."

"Right. But I agree with you, Marla would be a very annoying judge."

"Marla Dundee would be a very annoying *anything*," Fink said.

Fink took another handful of pretzels and shoved them in his mouth. This time, he finished chewing and swallowed before he spoke.

"Instead of making Marla a real judge, why don't we make her a *pretend* judge?" Fink suggested.

"What's a pretend judge?"

"A pretend judge is a judge whose opinion doesn't count."

"Won't it make Marla mad if her opinion doesn't count?" I asked.

"Not if she doesn't know."

"You mean Jessie would be our official judge and Marla would just kind of be along for the ride?" I asked.

"Exactly," said Fink.

So it was decided. We'd have two judges. One real and one pretend.

"Let's go inside and call Jessie right now and see if she wants to do it," said Fink.

We climbed down out of the tree, went inside, and got Jessie's number out of the class directory in the drawer under the cordless phone. I dialed the number as Fink and I walked upstairs to my room.

"Hello, Jessie? This is Nat," I said when she answered. "What do you mean, 'Nat who?' Give me a break! How many Nats do you know?"

Jessie immediately started rattling off famous Nats and Nathaniels.

"Nat King Cole, Nathaniel Webster —"

I interrupted and told her Fink was standing there with me, and we had something important we wanted to ask her.

"This better not be a phony phone call," she said. "What do you want?"

"We want to know if you'd like to be the official judge in a new game we've just invented," I said.

There was a long silence on the other end of the line.

"What kind of game is it?" she finally asked. "I don't have time for anything that involves juvenile activities, like punching each other in the arm, or seeing how far you can spit."

"There's no punching or spitting," I said. "I promise. You'll like this game. It's educational."

Fink gave me a big thumbs-up. He knew that was the right thing to say to get Jessie interested.

"What's this *educational* game called?" Jessie asked me.

I put my hand over the mouthpiece of the receiver.

"She wants to know what the game is called, Fink. Quick, think of something good!"

Fink thought for a second. "Tell her it's called . . . *Awesome Facts*!" he said.

I hesitated. "*Awesome*? Is that the best word you can come up with? It's kind of unoriginal."

"How about *Amazing Facts*?" he asked.

I wasn't thrilled with that, either. "We need a better word than *amazing* or *awesome*. Something you don't hear every day."

"*Outrageous?*" he suggested.

I shook my head. "Hang on a second, Jessie," I told her. I put the phone down and grabbed the thesaurus off the shelf over my desk. Fink came over to where I was standing and looked over my shoulder as I quickly turned to the word *amazing*. There were a lot of possibilities. *Surprising, incredible, astonishing, astounding* — the list went on and on, but nothing seemed quite right.

"How about *bodacious?*" asked Fink, pointing to one of the last words on the list.

Just then, Tallulah woke up from her nap and started running in her exercise wheel.

"That's it!" I said.

"What's it?" said Fink. "*Bodacious?*"

"No," I said. "Remember what Tallulah Treehaven always used to say to us when we were dancing?"

"You mean, 'Stop! I can't take it anymore!'?"

"No, not that. The thing she said when she *liked* how we were dancing."

"Oh, you mean, 'faboo!'" said Fink, imitating Miss Treehaven's funny voice.

"Yeah. The name of the game should be *Faboo Facts*. It's perfect!"

I picked up the phone. "Jessie?" I said. "The name of the game is —"

Fink grabbed the phone away from me and put his hand over the mouthpiece.

"Wait a second," he said, "I like *Bodacious Facts* better."

"No way! *Faboo Facts* is much better," I insisted. "It's way funnier."

"Who says the name should be funny?" asked Fink. "The facts aren't supposed to be funny, are they?"

"Hello! Hello?" Jessie's annoyed voice came out of the receiver in Fink's hand. Fink handed the phone back to me.

"Sorry, Jessie," I said. "I didn't mean to leave you hanging so long."

"So, what's the name of the game?" she said. "I told you, I don't have all day here."

"We're having a slight disagreement about what the name of the game should be," I explained.

"What are the choices? I'm supposed to be the judge, aren't I? Why don't you let *me* decide which one is better?"

That made sense. I told Fink Jessie wanted to decide for us, and he said that was fine with him.

"I'm telling you, though. She's going to go for *bodacious*. It's way more educational-sounding," he said.

"Okay, Jessie. Which name do you think is better? The choices are: *Faboo Facts* or *Bodacious Facts*," I told her.

"*Faboo?* That's Miss Treehaven's word, isn't it?"

"Imitation is the most sincere form of flattery," I said.

"Has anyone ever told you that you're totally weird, Nat?" asked Jessie.

"Only you," I said, "but it doesn't mean a whole lot coming from someone who's twice as weird as I am."

"If you think I'm so weird, then why are you asking me to be your judge?" asked Jessie.

Even though I couldn't actually see her, I knew that she had pushed her glasses up after that smarty-pants comment. But she had a point, and since I wanted her to agree to be our judge, I didn't bother to try to top her. Instead, I got back to the subject of naming our new game.

"So, what do you think, Jessie, *faboo* or *bodacious*?"

"*Bodacious*?" she said hesitantly. "Hmm, let me think about that one for a minute . . ."

Suddenly, I heard the unmistakable sound of pages flipping quickly on the other end of the phone. I clamped my hand over the receiver.

"She doesn't know what it means!" I said excitedly.

"What what means?" Fink asked.

"*Bodacious*. She doesn't know what it means!" I told him.

"Really? She admitted that?" Fink asked.

"No, but she's looking it up right now. I can hear her turning the pages of the dictionary. Listen!" I said, holding out the phone so that Fink could hear, too. He listened for a second and then broke into a huge grin.

Jessie is always trying to impress everybody by using big words when she talks. She thinks she has the most incredible vocabulary in the world. It drives Fink and me crazy. But we'd stumped her this time! And the best part was, we hadn't even been trying! True, neither one of us had known what *bodacious* meant either until just a second ago, but that didn't take away from our pleasure one bit.

"You do know what *bodacious* means, don't you, Jessie?" I said, unable to resist rubbing it in a little.

Fink snickered.

"Of course I know. Who doesn't?" Jessie asked, obviously stalling for time. "Everybody knows what it means."

"Really?" I said. "So what does it mean?"

"It means — um — it means —" She finally found what she'd been so desperately flipping those pages in search of. "It means 'remarkable or noteworthy.'"

It was obvious she'd read that right off the page. Even Jessie wouldn't use the word *noteworthy*.

"Oh, I'm so glad you know the word," I said with fake relief. "It would be a little embarrassing for you to have to judge a game that had a name you didn't understand, wouldn't it?"

Fink licked his finger and drew a line in the air.

"Score!" he shouted.

"Shh!" I said, laughing and putting my hand over the receiver again. "She'll hear you!"

"Listen, Nat," said Jessie. "I told you, I have better things to do than sit around listening to you and Fink blabber about some insignificant little game you've thought up. Just tell me what the judge is supposed to do, so I can decide if I want to do it."

"Okay, here's how it works: Fink and I each give you a fact and you have to judge which one is more interesting," I explained.

"That's it?" she said. "That's the whole game?"

"Yes."

"It's not very sophisticated."

"Maybe not, but you have to admit, it *is* educational. Just think of all the fascinating new facts you'll be learning."

She hesitated for a minute. "Okay. Fine. I'll do it. But on one condition."

Here it comes, I said to myself.

"I'll only be a judge if Marla can be a judge, too."

Bingo! I looked at Fink and smiled.

"Oh, sure, Jessie. No problem. We don't mind if Marla wants to be a judge, too," I said, "do we, Fink?"

Fink grinned again and shook his head. "Not at all," he said. "I don't know why we didn't think of that ourselves."

"When do we start?" asked Jessie.

"How about tomorrow morning?"

"Fine," said Jessie. "I'll tell Marla."

I was about to hang up when Fink grabbed the phone away from me.

"Wait! Jessie, don't hang up yet!" he shouted.

"What is it *now*?" she asked him.

"What did you decide the name of the game should be? You didn't tell us. Is it going to be *Faboo Facts* or *Bodacious Facts*?"

I could tell right away from the look on Fink's face what her decision had been. He hung up the phone.

"I can't believe it," he said.

"I told you *Faboo Facts* was a good name," I said.

"Yeah, but I was positive she would pick mine."

"I don't see why you're so surprised," I said. "You're not always right about everything, Fink."

"Almost always," he said. "And I was definitely right about this."

"Apparently you weren't, since she didn't happen to pick your name."

"Well, she should have," Fink said. "It was way better than yours."

"I'll bet nobody's ever accused you of having a lack of confidence, have they, Fink?" I asked.

"I just don't get it," Fink said, unable to let go of it. "*Bodacious Facts* is a much better name. Besides, it sounds more educational. How could she not have gone for that?"

"Did she say why she picked mine?"

"Yeah, she said she thought it was funnier and she liked that it was a little rated," Fink said.

"'A little rated'? What's that supposed to mean?"

"Beats me," said Fink. "Why do you care? She picked your name, didn't she?"

"You're not mad that she picked my name, are you?" I asked.

"Nah," he said, shaking his head. "I'm not mad. More like shocked. I'm not used to this feeling."

"What feeling?" I asked.

"Losing," he said. "You know me, Nat-o. I'm a born winner."

It's true. Fink doesn't lose very often. He's a pretty lucky person, I guess, but there's more to it than that. He believes in himself. Sometimes I wish I could be more like him.

"Hey, wasn't that great how Jessie didn't know what *bodacious* meant?" I said. "You should have heard little Miss Vocabulary trying to cover it up. It was hilarious."

I thought maybe reminding him of that would help get his mind off the name thing, but instead he looked even more upset.

"What's the matter?" I asked. "Are you really that freaked out that she didn't pick your name?"

"Yeah," he said. "But that's not what I'm worried

about at the moment. Right now, I'm more worried about *that*."

He was pointing at my leg. I hadn't even noticed, but I was scratching my knee.

"Uh-oh," I said.

If you know anything about me at all, you know that when my knee itches, it is definitely not a good sign.

CHAPTER THREE

Having an itchy knee that could predict the future and tell you how to avoid disasters would be terrific. Unfortunately, I don't have that kind of knee. My itchy knee can predict a disaster is coming, but it doesn't tell me when it's going to happen or what it's going to be, and since I don't know ahead of time, I can't do anything to try to avoid it.

"Why do you think it's itching this time?" asked Fink.

"I've told you a million times before, I never know why it's itching."

"Can't you at least *try* to figure it out?" asked Fink.

"Trust me, it won't work," I told him.

"How would you know unless you tried?" asked Fink.

"You're not going to tell me another story about George Washington Carver and his peanut butter, are you, Fink?"

"No, what I'm going to tell you is that you have to make a list."

"A list of what? All the annoying stories you've ever told me?" I asked. "That would take a pretty big piece of paper."

"Go ahead, make jokes if you want. But I'm telling you, I could help you figure out how to stay one step ahead of that itchy knee of yours if you'd just listen to me."

I shrugged. "Okay," I said, "I'll bite. What kind of list do I have to make?"

"A list of all the bad things you can think of, that could possibly be about to happen to you."

"*All* of the bad things that could possibly happen?" I asked. "There are way too many possibilities to list them all."

"So start by coming up with three," he said, grabbing a pencil and a sheet of paper off my desk.

"Okay. A giant jar of dill pickles could fall from the sky and hit me in the head. Then I'd lose my memory and wander around for years trying to figure out who I was."

"Come on, Nat-man," said Fink, "be serious. Name three bad things that could actually happen to you."

I thought for a minute. "Well, I suppose I could get another love note from Leslie Zebak. That would be bad."

"Excellent," said Fink as he wrote it down on his list. "Give me another."

"I could have another one of those dreams where Corn Bloomers shows up wearing a wedding dress."

"Now you're talking," said Fink. "One more."

"Oh, here's a definite possibility. I could fail the math test Mrs. West is giving us tomorrow. I really don't get that dividing fraction stuff at all, do you?" I asked as I reached down and scratched my knee.

"See!" shouted Fink, jumping out of his seat excitedly. "I knew this would work! You got itchy when you started talking about the math test. That's it! It's the math test."

"What are you so happy about, Fink? In case you've forgotten, it's not a good thing to fail a math test."

"You won't fail," said Fink. "Don't you get it? Now that we figured out that your knee is itching because of the test, all you have to do is study really hard and you'll outsmart the knee and pass. See? I told you this list-making thing would work. I am such a genius."

Like I said, a lack of confidence is not one of Fink's problems.

"Are you any good at dividing fractions?" I asked. "I think I might need a little help."

"I rule at dividing fractions," Fink said. "It's easy. All you have to do is remember to multiply one number by the recipro-something-or-other of whatever number comes after the division doo-hickey thing and you're there."

"That may sound easy to you, but I still don't get it."

"So, study the book," said Fink.

"Want to study with me?" I asked.

"No, I don't need to study. I'm totally solid on fractions," Fink said. "But since I'm such a nice guy, I'll keep you company while you study, if you want."

I spent the next forty-five minutes studying for the math test while Fink tore up paper towels and watched Tallulah use the strips to build a new nest in the corner of her cage.

"Do you want to stay for dinner?" I asked Fink when I felt that I finally understood the math well enough to close my book.

"No, thanks."

I wasn't surprised. Fink doesn't stay for dinner at my house very often because my mother sometimes makes him try a bite of whatever vegetable we're having, and she never serves dessert.

"I don't know how you can stand it," he tells me. "If you ask me, the whole point of eating dinner is getting to the dessert."

Actually, Fink ended up missing a pretty good dinner that night. My mom made her famous spaghetti sauce, which has a secret ingredient she won't tell anybody, even me. It was so good, I had two helpings.

"The way to a man's heart is through his stomach," my mother said as she heaped pasta and sauce on my plate.

Every time I think my mother's finally used up all the cornball expressions ever invented, she comes up with a new one I've never heard before.

"That's kind of gross when you think about it, Mom," I said. "Getting to somebody's heart through their stomach."

"Really? How so?" asked my mother.

But by then, my mouth was too full of spaghetti to say anything else.

Later, while my mom and I were clearing the table, I started thinking about the new game Fink and I had invented that day. It occurred to me that I could ask my mother if she knew any interesting facts that I might be able to use for round one of Faboo Facts.

"Interesting facts, huh?" she said. "Let's see. How about this — did you know that contrary to popular belief, George Washington's false teeth were not made of wood?"

"What were they made of?" I asked.

"They were probably made of some type of ivory or bone," she said.

"No offense, Mom, but is that really the most interesting fact you know?" I asked.

"At the moment, I think maybe that's the best I can do," she told me. "But I'll give it some thought in the morning when my mind is fresher and maybe I can come up with something better."

I loaded the dishwasher while my mom washed the pots and pans in the sink. She went upstairs to take a shower and I went into the den, flipped on the computer, and got online. I figured that was as good a place as any to start searching for an interesting fact.

Obviously, George Washington's teeth were not nearly *faboo* enough for our game, but they did give me an idea. I thought maybe there might be other, more interesting things about teeth that I could use. I did a couple of searches and came up with a site about teeth, hair, and fingernails. I read a bunch of things and narrowed it down to two choices. Fact number one: The Egyptians made their toothpaste out of vinegar and stones. Fact number two: If you weave ten thousand human hairs together, it will make a rope strong enough to pick up a car.

I decided the hair fact was the best one. I wrote it down on a slip of paper and put it in the front pocket of my backpack, along with my snack money. Then I took one last look at my math book to make sure the fraction stuff had completely sunk in, brushed my teeth — with my vinegarless and stone-free toothpaste — and went to bed.

The next morning, Fink was waiting for me on the corner as usual. I was glad to see him, because I had something important to tell him.

"I figured out what Jessie meant yesterday when she said that the name *Faboo Facts* was a little rated," I said as we started walking.

"Oh, yeah? What?" asked Fink.

"She didn't say 'a little rated,' she said 'alliterated.' Remember when we did our poetry unit with

Mrs. West? *Alliteration* is when two words start with the same sound. Ffff-aboo Ffff-acts. Get it? Two Fs."

Fink looked at me and blinked quickly a couple of times. "You are such a ffff-reak sometimes, Natalie," he said.

Of all the nicknames Fink has given me over the years, that's definitely my least favorite.

"Hey, don't blame me, Fink. Jessie's the one who said it," I reminded him. "I was just translating for you."

We crossed Buckingham at the light and started up Needham Road.

"How's your knee today?" Fink asked me.

"Fine, at the moment."

"I'm telling you, it was the math test that was making you itch," he said. "Now that you've studied for the test, you won't be itching again. I'm positive."

"I hope you're right," I said.

"Of course I'm right," said Fink. "So, did you find a good fact?"

"I think so. Did you?"

"Absolutely," he said. "Mine rocks."

"Where did you get it?"

"You think I'm going to tell *you*?" he said. "You're the enemy."

"The *enemy*? Hey, I thought this was a game, not a war."

"Relax," said Fink, "all I meant was that you're the competition. You don't expect me to give my secret source away to the competition, do you?"

"I guess not."

My knee had started itching again, and I bent down to scratch it.

"I'll bet you're thinking about that math test right now, aren't you?" asked Fink.

"I don't think so, but maybe. I'm still a little nervous about it, I guess."

"You know what your problem is, Nat-man? You lack confidence. Trust me on this. We're both going to ace that test today. You'll see. You just have to think positive. Meanwhile, quit worrying about it and try thinking about something else instead," Fink suggested.

"Like what?"

"Like, when do you want to play the game?"

"I don't care," I said, resisting the urge to scratch again, even though my knee was really itchy now. "I guess if Jessie is there early enough, we could do it before school. Otherwise, how about after lunch?"

"Sounds good to me," said Fink.

We ran into Jeremy Huan and Danny Lebson. They were standing on the sidewalk pointing at something up in a tree.

"What are you guys looking at?" asked Fink.

"Squirrel fight," said Jeremy.

Just then, two squirrels came scrambling down the trunk of the tree, down into the grass where they started running around in circles.

"Why are they fighting?" I asked.

"The big one's got a nut and the little one wants it," said Danny.

The larger squirrel had a black spot on his back, and I saw that Danny was right; he had some kind of nut in his mouth. Whenever he stopped running, he'd turn around to face the smaller squirrel, and holding the nut tightly in his front paws, he'd chatter at his attacker in a way that almost sounded like he was laughing at him. The little one would come running up to try to snatch the nut away, but right when he got there, the big one would pop the nut back in his mouth and take off again.

"Which one do you think is going to win?" Fink asked.

"It's obvious," I said. "The big one."

"Definitely," said Jeremy. "He's already got the nut. Plus, watch him run. He's much more coordinated than that little squirrel."

"Being well coordinated isn't everything," said Fink. "I'm putting my money on the little guy."

"Are you kidding?" asked Danny. "Why? He's a wimp. A total loser."

"He may look like a wimp, but I'll bet he's got a big brain hiding under all that fur. He's probably coming up with a brilliant plan to fake out the big squirrel and trick him into dropping the nut so he can swoop in and grab it for himself — you watch."

But as we stood there and watched, the squirrel

with the black spot on his back finally got tired of the game, and using his strong, well-coordinated back legs, he kicked the little squirrel in the face and sent him flying. Then he climbed up the tree and sat on a high branch. While the little squirrel looked up at him sadly from the ground below, the big squirrel expertly split the nut open, gobbled it down, and as a final insult, dropped the empty shells down on the little squirrel's head.

"What a loser," laughed Danny.

"Guess his brain's not so big after all, huh, Fink?" said Jeremy.

"Well, he *should* have won," Fink said. "I'd still put my money on him any day."

"A fool and his money are soon parted," I said.

"Do you have an expression for *every* situation?" asked Fink. "Even betting on squirrel fights?"

"Unfortunately, yes," I told him.

Because we'd stopped to watch the squirrels, we got to school a little later than usual. The first bell had already rung and everybody else had gone inside. When we got to the classroom, Jessie and Marla were standing by the door checking their mailboxes for homework sheets and notices.

"You guys are late," Jessie said. "If you'd gotten here on time, we could have had the contest already."

"What contest?" asked Jeremy.

"It's not really a contest," I said. "It's more of a game."

"So, when do you want to do it?" asked Jessie.

"After lunch, I guess," said Fink.

"Can Jer and I play, too?" asked Danny.

"No," said Fink, "it's just between Nat and me."

"And I get to be the judge," said Jessie.

"Hey, I'm judging, too, aren't I?" said Marla. "I've been in court lots of times to watch my dad. I know tons about courtrooms. I plan to be a lawyer myself someday, you know."

"I thought you wanted to be a ballerina," said Jeremy, getting up on his toes and doing a funny dance just like the one Tallulah does when I hold a treat over her head.

"I can do both," said Marla, putting her hands on her hips and sticking out her chin.

41

"Oh, sure. I know lots of lawyers who wear tutus to court," said Fink.

"You didn't even know what a tutu was until I told you, Boyd Fink," said Marla.

Actually, that was true. Marla had told Fink and me that we were going to have to wear tutus when we danced with Tallulah Treehaven. Luckily, that hadn't turned out to be true.

I checked my mailbox. No stinky love notes from Leslie, so it didn't look like that was what my knee had been warning me about.

"Ladies and gentlemen, please take your seats," said Mrs. West.

"Let's meet right after lunch, out on the wooden bench," said Fink. "Okay?"

"Can we at least watch?" asked Danny.

"Maybe, but you can't vote," said Fink. "Only Jessie gets to vote."

"Hey!" objected Marla.

"And Marla," Fink quickly added, even though we both knew it wasn't true.

We all went and sat down at our desks. After she took attendance, Mrs. West told us to clear our desks and get ready for the math test. My palms started sweating, but I noticed that my knee wasn't itching. Maybe Fink was right, and all that studying had paid off. Or maybe my own knee was playing tricks on me, making me think I was going to do okay on the test when all along it knew that I was going to bomb.

Well, whether I wanted to or not, I was about to find out.

CHAPTER FOUR

There were ten problems on the test and I was able to solve them all pretty easily. I couldn't believe how quickly I had finished. I checked my answers twice before I handed it in.

"That test was really easy, didn't you think?" I asked Fink later as we were walking to the cafeteria at lunchtime.

"Totally," Fink said. "I told you we would ace it."

"Do you really think we did?"

"Of course we did, Nat-o-matica," he said.

It must be really nice to be that sure of yourself.

We didn't talk about the math test or about Faboo Facts while we ate, but I noticed Fink patting his shirt pocket a couple of times. I figured he'd probably written his fact down on a slip of paper, too, put it in his pocket, and was checking to make sure it was still there.

"Are you done?" Fink asked as he took the last bite of his sandwich.

"Done," I said.

Fink balled up his napkin and tried to shoot it into the wastebasket. He missed by a mile. Fink is great at a lot of things, but not sports. I crumpled up the empty bag from my chips and tossed it over my shoulder into the trash can.

"Lucky shot," said Fink.

"That's not luck, that's skill," I said. "Watch it and weep — left-handed this time."

I picked up my milk carton, stood up, and made another perfect shot.

"How do you do that?" asked Fink.

I shrugged. "Practice makes perfect," I said.

Fink picked up his milk carton, which was still half full.

"Left-handed and with my eyes closed. *You* watch

it and weep!" he said as he tossed the carton over his shoulder.

Unfortunately, instead of going into the trash, Fink's milk carton sailed across the room and landed with a wet *plonk!* in about the worst place possible: right on Mad Dog's head! That's right. Fink had just hit Mad Dog Ditmeyer, the biggest, meanest kid in the whole school.

"Who did that?" he roared, jumping out of his seat so fast his chair went flying.

Everyone froze. Milk dripped down Mad Dog's face as he slowly scanned the room, looking for the guilty party.

"I said, who did that?" Mad Dog shouted again.

Still no one moved.

Fink, as I've already said, is a very confident person. However, at those rare times when he's not feeling completely sure of himself, and especially if he's scared, he sometimes does something very strange. He laughs. And that's what he did right then.

"Shh! Knock it off, Fink," I whispered. "Quit laughing or he's going to know it was you."

But Fink couldn't control himself. Once he started giggling, he just couldn't stop. Of course, Mad Dog heard him.

"Big mistake, Fink. BIG mistake," he said. "Hey, everybody! Guess what's for dessert today? Cream of Fink pie!" And he balled his giant hands into two huge fists and jumped up onto the lunchroom table. "Prepare to be creamed!"

"Run, Fink!" I shouted as I grabbed my jacket off the back of my chair and ran for the door.

Mad Dog started jumping from one table to the next, like a giant frog leaping from lily pad to lily pad, chasing Fink. Fink is a pretty fast runner, but I think the fact that he couldn't stop his nervous laughter really slowed him down. Mad Dog caught up with him just as he reached the door.

"It was an accident!" Fink yelled. "I was aiming for the trash can, honest." Mad Dog grabbed Fink's arm and started to twist it behind his back.

"Let him go!" I shouted as I pushed him off of Fink. "He didn't do it on purpose, Mad Dog. Everybody knows he's got crummy aim."

"Like I said, Finky boy," Mad Dog growled as he lunged at Fink, grabbing for his arm again, "prepare to get creamed."

I could tell Fink was completely terrified and I didn't blame him. I've always been afraid of Mad Dog. Believe me, when he says he's going to cream you, he means it. I ought to know — he's been on my case big-time ever since my mom put his braces on.

"Don't hurt me," Fink begged between nervous giggles. "Please don't hurt me."

"You didn't really think you could get away with something like that without getting paid back, did you?" he asked. "Just ask your little buddy here. Does Mad Dog pay back, or does Mad Dog pay back?"

"Mad Dog definitely pays back," I said quickly. "But he didn't mean to hit you with the milk, Mad Dog. He's sorry. Aren't you, Fink? Tell him you're sorry."

"I'm sorry, Mad Dog," Fink said.

"Sorry's not good enough, Finky boy. Not after what you did," said Mad Dog, shaking his head.

Almost everybody had left the lunchroom as soon

as Mad Dog had started yelling, but there were a few people, including Jeremy and Danny, who'd hung around to see what would happen.

"My money's on Mad Dog," I heard Jeremy say.

"Mine too," said Danny.

Poor Fink. Everyone was betting against him, just the way we had that morning with the little squirrel. But, unlike the little squirrel, who ended up all alone with nutshells on his head, Fink had a friend to help him out.

"Come on, Mad Dog. Fink said he was sorry. What else do you want him to say?" I asked.

Mad Dog always has a mean look on his face, but when he smiles, like he did right then, he looks even meaner.

"If I tell you what I want you to say, do you promise that you'll say it?" he asked Fink.

Fink looked at me and I nodded. I know from experience that whenever possible, it's best to give Mad Dog his way.

"Okay, I promise," said Fink.

"Swear on your mother's spit?" asked Mad Dog.

"That's gross, but yes, I swear on my mother's spit," said Fink.

"Good. Now, repeat after me: *I, Boyd Fink.*"

"I, Boyd Fink," said Fink nervously.

"*Am a total wuss,*" said Mad Dog.

"Am a total wuss," repeated Fink.

"*And I bow down.*"

"And I bow down."

"*Before the king.*"

"Before the king," said Fink.

"Now get down on your knees and kiss my shoe," said Mad Dog.

"WHAT?" said Fink.

"Kiss it or die," said Mad Dog, balling up his fists again.

Everyone who was watching was completely silent. Would he do it? Would he actually kiss Mad Dog's shoe — a shoe that had walked through, and stepped in, who knows what? Not to mention, it was a shoe that had carried Mad Dog's stinky foot around inside it for weeks! I felt my stomach lurch and for a minute I thought maybe I was going to lose my lunch.

Did Fink kiss it? I think he probably would have. But in the end, just as he puckered up his lips and bent down over Mad Dog's shoe, Mr. Cappart, the vice principal of our school, showed up to see what was going on.

"Is there a problem here, Douglas?" he asked Mad Dog.

"A problem?" said Mad Dog. "No, sir, not really. Clumsy old Fink here just tripped and fell down and I was giving him a hand up. Isn't that right, Finky boy?"

Fink started giggling again. "That's right," he said. "He's just helping me up, Mr. Cappart."

Mad Dog reached down and helped Fink stand up. Of course, Mr. Cappart didn't know the reason Fink was giggling was because he was scared stiff. So, instead of hauling Mad Dog down to his office for detention, he smiled and patted him on the back.

"That's what I call good citizenship," said Mr. Cappart. "I'm very happy to see that, especially coming from you, Douglas. Now, why don't you all head out to the yard for a little fresh air before the bell rings." Mr. Cappart held the door open for us as we all filed out into the yard.

"Are you okay?" I asked Fink as soon as we were outside.

"What do you think?" he asked. "He made me call myself a wuss in front of everybody. Would you be okay?"

"At least you didn't actually kiss his shoe," I said.

"Yeah, but I came pretty close. And don't you dare say anything about close only counting in horse shows."

"Horse*shoes*," I said.

"You know, what just happened in there is partly your fault," Fink said.

My fault? I was the only one who'd taken his side and tried to help him out. How could he possibly blame me?

"You told me to agree to whatever Mad Dog said," Fink explained.

"I told you to *say* whatever he said, not *do* whatever he said, Fink," I said. "Actually, I probably still would have told you to do whatever he said, too, if you'd asked me. He was pretty mad! I mean, you *did* hit him in the head with a milk carton. You don't think that was my fault, too, do you?"

"No, but it's definitely the last time I'll ever take advice from you. I should have known better. I know how you are."

"What does that mean?" I asked.

"You let things happen to you without doing anything about it, Nat-o. Your knee itches and you don't even try to figure out why. Mad Dog throws spitballs at you, and you just duck. But that's YOU, not ME. I'm a fighter. I'm a winner."

I knew that Fink was just letting off steam because he was embarrassed about what had happened with Mad Dog, but that didn't make it any easier to hear him put me down.

"Hey, you guys, we've been waiting over here forever. Hurry up!"

I'd forgotten all about the game. Jessie and Marla were calling to us from the bench, but I had no interest in playing anymore.

"Let's forget about the game for now, Fink," I said. "I don't think either one of us is in the mood."

"Speak for yourself. I'm totally in the mood for the game," said Fink. "In fact, beating you right now would cheer me up big-time."

I didn't want to play, but I also didn't want to cross Fink. The guy had almost been forced to kiss Mad Dog's shoe. If Fink thought that playing the game would make him feel better, I figured I should do that for him.

"What took you guys so long?" Jessie asked when we got to the bench. "Did something happen in there?"

Fink shot me a look. "Nothing happened," he said. "We both ate big lunches today and it just took us a little longer to finish, that's all." Then he rubbed his stomach and forced out a loud burp to make it seem like he was telling the truth.

"Gross," said Jessie.

"Yes, you are," said Fink.

"I'm not even going to dignify that with a response," said Jessie, pushing up her glasses.

"This bench is perfect for us," Marla said, patting the bench, "because real judges sit on benches."

"Everybody sits on benches," said Fink.

"For your information, the big, high desks that judges sit at, the ones they pound those wooden hammers on, are called *benches*," Marla explained, in her usual annoying way. Then she turned to Jessie and added, "Did you ever notice that not only are boys rude but they also know nothing?"

"For your information, those wooden hammers judges bang on their benches are called *gavels*," I said.

Marla blushed. "I knew that. I was just trying to make it easier for you to understand," she said, "that's all."

"Yeah, right," said Fink.

"You know," said Jessie, "some people might not think it's very wise to insult the judges right before they're supposed to make a decision."

"I'm not worried," Fink said. "My fact is going

to blow Nat's fact right out of the water, no matter what. Come on, let's play."

"Okay," said Jessie. "You start, Fink."

"Hey, wait a minute," Marla interrupted. "How come you get to decide who goes first?"

"Because I'm the head judge."

"I thought we were supposed to make all the decisions together. That's what you said," said Marla.

"Okay, as the head judge, I think that Fink should start. *Do you agree?*" And it was very clear from the tone of her voice that Marla had better agree with Jessie if she knew what was good for her.

"I agree. You may proceed, Mr. Fink," said Marla, turning to Fink. She probably picked up that "proceed" thing from her dad. Or from watching lawyer shows on TV. Either way, like almost everything Marla says, it was annoying.

Fink reached into his pocket — the one he'd been patting earlier — and pulled out a folded square of paper. He unfolded it and cleared his throat. "I hope you're ready, because this fact I have here is so amazing, it will curl your hair. So incredible, it will make your mouth pop open and your tongue hang out like a dog in the sun. So *bodacious,* it will boggle your mind like it's never been boggled before."

"Spit it out!" said Jessie impatiently. "The bell's going to ring soon."

"You're sure you're ready?" asked Fink, trying to draw out the suspense a little longer. "Because, I'm telling you, this is no ordinary fact. This fact is so —"

"TELL US ALREADY!" shouted Marla.

Fink looked at the piece of paper in his hand and cleared his throat again.

"Sea turtles cry when they lay their eggs," he said.

Marla was the first to react. "You made that up," she snorted. "Everybody knows turtles can't cry."

"Yes, they can," said Fink. "It's a fact."

"It is not," said Marla. "You obviously made that up. I *had* a turtle and I can tell you, for a fact, that it never cried."

"I'd cry if I was your pet," said Fink.

"You're out of order!" shouted Marla.

"Oh, yeah? Well, you're a pain in the neck know-it-all who doesn't really know anything," Fink said.

"What are the rules here?" asked Jessie, turning to me. "Do you have to be able to prove that your fact is true or not?"

"We don't have rules yet," I said.

"I think you should have to prove it. Otherwise, Marla is right; you guys could just make stuff up," Jessie said.

"That's right," said Marla, clearly pleased that Jessie was agreeing with her. "You could just make stuff up — like, for instance, about sea turtles crying."

"I didn't make it up! I can prove it!" said Fink. "I've got a book on sea turtles at home and it says in there that when sea turtles lay their eggs, saltwater comes out of their eyes to help keep the sand out."

"It says that saltwater comes out of their eyes?" asked Marla. "Are you sure?"

"Yes! It's right there in black and white. I'll show you. I can bring the book in tomorrow."

"Does the book say they actually cry?" asked Jessie.

"It says saltwater comes out of their eyes. What

do you want? Tears are saltwater, aren't they?" asked Fink.

"Well, yes," said Jessie, "but crying is when saltwater comes out of your eyes because you're sad."

"Or happy," said Marla. "Some people cry because they're happy."

"Would you be happy if you had to lay a hundred eggs with sand in your eyes?" asked Fink.

"The point is not whether the turtles are happy or sad, it's whether or not you can say that when the saltwater comes out of their eyes, they're *crying*," said Jessie.

"What would you call it?" asked Fink. "Laughing?"

"Very funny. Let's hear Nat's fact," said Jessie. "We can decide about the turtles later if we have to."

I had a bad feeling about the way this was going. The only reason I had agreed to play was because Fink had insisted he wanted to. But it was too late to back out now. I unzipped the front pocket of my backpack, pulled out the slip of paper, and read. "If you weave ten thousand human hairs together, it will make a rope that is strong enough to lift a car."

One of the reasons we chose Jessie to be the judge in the first place is that she's not afraid to say what she thinks. She didn't even hesitate before making her decision.

"Nat wins."

CHAPTER FIVE

*

Both Marla and Fink started yelling at once.

"You're supposed to ask me what I think before you make any official decisions!" shouted Marla. "That doesn't count. Nat isn't the winner yet, because I haven't voted."

"She's right. Your decision is bogus!" said Fink.

So much for Marla being a pretend judge. Fink certainly seemed to care about her opinion now.

"My fact is better than his," he went on. "Besides, how come you didn't ask him to prove his? Have you ever seen someone try to pick up a car with a hairy rope? Come on!"

"We're supposed to be partners!" Marla shouted at Jessie. "It's not fair. You promised."

In the middle of all the yelling and complaining, Jessie bent down and took off her right shoe. She started pounding it on the arm of the bench until Fink and Marla were finally quiet.

"First of all, the reason I didn't ask Nat to prove his fact is that I happen to know the hair thing is true. I've read it somewhere before. Second of all, I'm sorry, Marla. I guess I should have asked you first, before I said anything about who the winner was, but Nat's fact is obviously more interesting than Fink's. *Don't you agree?*"

There it was again, that tone in Jessie's voice that made it clear that Marla had to agree with her. So, of course, she did.

"Nat wins," Marla said.

The bell rang then, and we had to go inside. I was happy that I'd won, but I didn't make a big deal out of it or anything. Fink's day was going badly enough without any help from me.

"That was totally bogus," he grumbled as we walked together toward the front door.

"Well, don't be mad at me," I said as we walked up the steps. "I'm not the one who decided the winner. Jessie did. Besides, it's just a game."

"I know it's just a game," he said, "but that doesn't mean it wasn't bogus. My fact was obviously better. They just voted against me because I was kidding around before the contest."

I opened the door and we went in. Fink was walking next to me with his head down and both hands jammed into his pockets.

"Are you sure you're not mad at me?" I asked again.

"Not yet, but I'm going to be if you keep asking me that," he said.

"I never knew that turtles cried," I said, hoping to smooth things over between us a little. "That's definitely a cool fact. It's at least as cool as the hairy rope, if you ask me."

"Yeah? If you think that's cool, just wait 'til you

see what I come up with for tomorrow," Fink said with a laugh. "I'm definitely going to out-faboo you."

"If you say so," I said.

"Oh, I say so, all right," he said, "and I mean so, too. I'm beating you if it's the last thing I do."

"Fine," I said.

"Way fine," he said.

I let it drop after that because the whole conversation was beginning to make me very uncomfortable. Fink is not usually a bad sport. Although he and I can both be competitive sometimes, we're never that way with each other. We're always on the same team, the same side. At least, that's how it had always been up until we started playing Faboo Facts. I leaned over and scratched my knee.

"Hey, how come you're still itching?" asked Fink. "The math test is over."

"Maybe I didn't do as well on it as I thought," I said. "Maybe that's why I'm still itchy."

"Well, I'm sure I aced it, and you said you thought it was easy, so you probably did okay, too."

It turned out Fink was right. At the end of the day,

Mrs. West stood at the door and handed our tests back to us as we filed out of the classroom. Not only did I do okay, I got a perfect score!

"You were right! I aced that puppy, thanks to you," I told Fink happily as we started walking home.

"Me? What did I do?" he asked me.

"You told me to outsmart my knee and study for the test. Don't you remember?" I asked. "If I hadn't done that, I would have flunked, for sure. I owe it all to you!"

"Glad I could help," he said, but he didn't sound all that glad.

He'd had a pretty bad day. Maybe acing a math test wasn't enough to make him forget about losing at Faboo Facts and almost kissing Mad Dog's shoe.

We walked in silence for a while, which was very unusual for us. When Fink and I are together, we usually don't stop talking except to eat, and sometimes even that doesn't stop us.

"Listen, I'm planning to teach Tallulah how to do another trick this afternoon," I said as we came around the corner and started to walk up our street.

"I was thinking maybe I could teach her how to roll over. You want to come over to my house and help?"

"Nah," he said, "I have to practice for my clarinet lesson. My teacher called my mom last night and told her my playing is 'appalling.'"

"*Appalling* means bad, right?" I asked.

"Yeah. According to her, I'm just as bad as I was when I started taking lessons. You've heard me play. Do you think it's true?"

"Um . . . I'm not very musical myself, so I'm probably the wrong person to ask," I said.

But Fink and I both knew I was fudging. It was true. I'd been to a couple of his recitals, so I knew. He was awful when he started, and he's just as awful now. I took piano lessons for a while myself, but the difference between Fink and me is that when it turned out that I was appalling, my mom let me quit taking lessons. She's not very musical, either, so she said she'd sort of expected it.

"The apple doesn't fall far from the tree," she told me.

Fink's parents are both very musical. His mom sings solos in the church choir and his dad plays the guitar. But in Fink's case, somehow the apple managed to break the rules and fall a long way from the tree — at least when it comes to playing the clarinet.

I found a little gray pebble on the sidewalk and started kicking it along in front of me as we walked. Fink stuck his foot out and tried to kick it away from me, but he tripped over his own feet and would have fallen down if I hadn't caught him by the elbow.

"Are you okay?" I asked him.

"Quit asking me that, will you?" he said, pulling his elbow away with a jerk. "There's nothing wrong with me. I'm *fine*, okay? I just tripped."

"Chill out," I said. "I was only trying to save you from breaking your neck."

"The last time you tried to save me, I made the mistake of listening to you, and look where it got me!" said Fink.

We had reached Fink's house, which is two houses down the block from mine, on the opposite side of the street. He was acting like a total turkey, but I thought maybe if we could talk about it, he might snap out of his crummy mood.

"Are you sure you don't want to come over?" I asked.

"I'm sure. See you later," he said. "And don't forget to bring another fact tomorrow. I'm going to out-faboo you if it's the last thing I do."

"Yeah, I know, you told me already," I said. "But don't you think maybe we should drop the game for now? I mean, at least until you're feeling a little better?"

"I told you, I'm fine. And I'm dying for another shot at you," Fink said.

My knee suddenly itched and I bent down to scratch it. Fink noticed, but he didn't say anything. He just shook his head.

"I guess it wasn't the math test that was making me itch after all, huh?" I said.

"Guess not," he said. "Unless, for some sick reason, now you're worrying about the fact that you aced it."

"I doubt that," I said. "I feel great about it. So why do you think I'm itching?"

"How should I know?" said Fink as he turned to walk away. "But if I were you, I'd try to figure it out fast, before something bad happens."

As I crossed the street and started walking toward my house, I thought about what Fink had just said and also about what he'd said earlier, about how I was the kind of person who just let things happen. It kind of bugged me. I'm not as sure of myself as Fink is, but I'm not a wimp, either. I decided then and there to prove to myself, and to Fink, that I was the kind of person who could get to the bottom of things. One way or another, I would figure out what this itch was all about!

When I got home, I passed by the window of my mom's office. She was working on a patient, but she looked up and waved to me to come inside.

My mom's office is attached to our house. Most of her patients are around my age, of course, because that's when most kids get braces, but she has a few patients who are grown-ups, too. The woman sitting in the examination chair that day happened to be one of them, Mrs. Townsend.

Mrs. Townsend is very — well, *round*. She has big round eyes, and a round red face, and her body looks like a big round rubber ball with short little arms and legs sticking out of it. She reminds me of a Christmas ornament I once made by poking toothpicks into a styrofoam ball. Mrs. Townsend also happens to be Fink's clarinet teacher.

"Hello, Nathaniel," she said when I came into the office. "How are you? My goodness, you're growing like a weed! Or should I say *reed*. Get it? Like a clarinet reed?" She giggled.

"Hi, Mrs. Townsend," I said with a little wave.

"The reason I called you in here, honey," my mom said, "is that I just mentioned to Mrs. Townsend, not two seconds ago, that you are collecting interesting facts, and she says she has a good one for you."

"Really?" I said, wondering what someone like Mrs. Townsend might think was interesting. It would probably have something to do with music.

"Did you know, Nathaniel, that the largest ice

cream sundae on record was made in Alberta, Canada, and it weighed over twenty-four tons?" she told me, sitting forward in the chair.

"Wow. Twenty-four tons? That's a lot of ice cream," I said.

"It certainly is," Mrs. Townsend said dreamily, lying back again.

Considering her roundness, I guess I shouldn't have been surprised that Mrs. Townsend's interesting fact came with whipped cream and a cherry on top.

"Can you prove it?" I asked, remembering the problem Fink had run into with the crying turtles.

"Can I prove it?" Mrs. Townsend laughed. "I was there! I was second in command of the hot-fudge brigade. What a glorious experience that was — being up to my elbows in chocolate. Can you imagine? The whole town was involved, even the mayor. He got to put the cherry on top. The event was months in the making, and when it was over, I remember we all fell into a terrible funk."

"What's a funk?" I asked.

"The best way I can think of to describe it is that

you feel as though you've fallen off the merry-go-round, and life has left you behind. Sudden hot-fudge withdrawal can do that to a person, believe you me," she said seriously. Then she winked at me and laughed, which made all three of her chins jiggle.

I thanked Mrs. Townsend for her interesting fact, kissed my mom quickly on the cheek, left the office, and went into the house. I headed straight for the kitchen, where I got a handful of carrot sticks out of the fridge, popped a bag of microwave popcorn, grabbed a chunk of cheddar cheese, and went upstairs to get Tallulah started on her new trick.

"You ready, girl?" I asked Tallulah as I took her out of the tank and held her up so that our noses touched. Her whiskers tickled my nose and I laughed.

For the next hour, I tried my best to teach Tallulah how to roll over, but no matter how much cheese I offered her, she refused to do it. I even tried demonstrating it on the floor myself, but she wasn't interested. Finally I gave up and put her back in the cage.

"You think rolling over is hard?" I asked her. "Fink thinks I should try to teach you how to read."

I got all my homework done and was about to start looking for a new (good) fact, when once again my knee started to itch. I remembered the promise I'd made myself, and decided it was time to take action.

Whenever we do science experiments in class, Mrs. West has us make a data log. We draw a bunch of columns with headings, and then list all the stuff we find out, so that we can look at the log later and draw conclusions about the experiments we've done.

I turned to a blank page in my notebook and drew lines on it, making seven columns, one for each day of the week. Then I drew lines across the page and wrote: *TIME, PLACE, PEOPLE, SUBJECT*.

I sat back, closed my eyes, and tried to remember everything about when the itching had occurred. It had started the day before, when Fink and I had been standing in my room. We'd just finished asking Jessie if she wanted to be the judge, so it was probably around four o'clock. I wrote all of that information in the *MONDAY* column. Then under *PEOPLE* I wrote *Fink, Tallulah,* and *Jessie*. Even though Tallulah isn't a person and Jessie had only been there on the phone, I figured I might as well include them.

Under *SUBJECT* I put *Faboo Facts,* because that's what we'd been talking to Jessie about on the phone. But then I remembered that later that same day, Fink had first suggested I was itching because of the math test. So I put *Math Test* in that square, too. That took care of *MONDAY*.

When I started filling in *TUESDAY*, it got confusing. I knew I had itched several times that day, but it was hard to remember the details. I put *Math Test* again, but then I crossed it out because I hadn't itched at all during the test — only before and after. What else had I been thinking about?

I was interrupted by the phone ringing. I was hoping it was Fink, calling to say he wasn't grumpy anymore. I wanted to tell him that I was taking his advice and trying to figure out the cause of my itching. Also, Fink has a good memory, so I thought maybe he could help me remember more details.

"Hello?" I said, catching it in the middle of the third ring.

But it wasn't Fink, it was Jessie. "Listen, I've decided the rule is, from now on, you guys have to bring proof with you to school, or your fact will be automatically disqualified," she said.

"You know, Jessie, just because you're the judge, it doesn't mean you get to go around making up rules whenever you feel like it. Fink and I are the ones who invented the game. We should be the ones who make the rules."

"Fine, be that way. I don't want to judge your silly game, anyway," Jessie said, and she started to hang up.

"Wait!" I said. "I didn't say you shouldn't be the judge, I just said you shouldn't be the one making up the rules."

"I don't care who makes the rule, but I'm telling you, there needs to be a rule that says there has to be proof. It's not a big deal. Just bring in the book and show it to us!"

"What if we didn't get the fact from a book? What if we got it off the Internet?" I asked. "What are we supposed to do, bring in our computers?"

"Don't be dim. If you get it off the Internet, just

bring the web address. That way, Marla or I can check it later."

I thought about Mrs. Townsend's ice cream sundae. How would I prove that was true, bring Fink's clarinet teacher to school with me?

"Can't you just trust us, Jessie?" I asked. "It would be so much easier that way. Fink and I are not going to make up facts. We're best friends, we wouldn't lie to each other. Besides, it's just a game."

"I can't help it if I take my judicial responsibilities seriously," said Jessie. "But I suppose if you're willing to promise that your facts are real, I guess maybe that will have to do."

Judicial responsibilities? That was *so* Jessie.

After I hung up, I started to dial Fink's number. I wanted to tell him about Jessie's phone call and see how he was doing. I got to the third number and I had to stop. My knee was itching again! I grabbed my log and started writing.

Mile in past field," he said, pointing a foil...
directed sunstruck to they...however to the for a girl
know the water anthony."

CHAPTER SIX

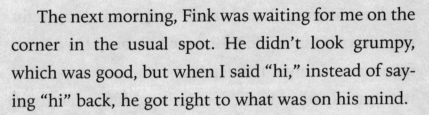

The next morning, Fink was waiting for me on the corner in the usual spot. He didn't look grumpy, which was good, but when I said "hi," instead of saying "hi" back, he got right to what was on his mind.

"So, do you have it?" he asked.

"Have what?"

"Your fact," said Fink.

"Yeah," I said, "I've got it."

Between trying to teach Tallulah to roll over, making my itch log, and doing my homework, I hadn't had any time to look for more facts, so I'd decided to go ahead and use Mrs. Townsend's ice cream sundae.

Fink touched his pocket and smiled.

"Mine is right here," he said, "and it's a total winner — guaranteed to blow whatever you've got right out of the water. *Kaboom!*"

"Hang on," I said, putting my backpack down on the sidewalk in front of me so I could dig around in it. I pulled out my notebook and a stubby pencil and turned to my log.

"What are you doing?" asked Fink.

"I started this log yesterday, to keep track of when my knee itches," I told him, "and it's itching right now. It's only going to take a second, but I have to fill it in before I forget the details."

I quickly filled in the log, writing down that I was outside on the corner of Huron Avenue and Nichols Street and that the only people around were some guy mowing his lawn, Fink, and some squirty little kindergartners walking to school holding hands.

"How come you decided to make a log?" asked Fink.

"I don't know. I guess because of what you said yesterday about what kind of person I am."

"Don't worry about what I said, Nat-o. I was just

crabbed out. You're fine just the way you are. If you want something to worry about, though, you should worry about this," and he patted his shirt pocket. "I've got a winner today."

"Yeah, you told me — *Kaboom!*"

I was glad when Fink said he liked me the way I am. It made me feel better, but I was worried about playing the game. What if I won and he got mad all over again? I wished there was a way to get out of playing, but I could tell from the way he kept patting that pocket — Fink couldn't wait for round two to begin. *Kaboom!*

Since there was no squirrel fight to slow us down, we got to school that morning before the bell rang. Jessie and Marla were already there.

"Got your facts?" Marla called over to us. "Because the judges are ready!"

"Come on," said Fink. "It's time for you to be outfabooed, Natalie."

My knee was itching, but I wasn't sure if it was left over from when we'd been on Huron Avenue, or if this was a new itch. Either way, there wasn't time to fill out another log entry, so I reluctantly followed Fink over to the bench where Jessie and Marla were waiting.

"Marla and I discussed it," said Jessie, "and this time, to be fair, we've decided that Nat should give his fact first."

"Okay," I said, pulling the piece of paper I'd written my fact on out of my backpack. "The largest ice cream sundae in history was made in Alberta, Canada, and it weighed over twenty-four tons."

"Can you prove it?" asked Marla.

"Oh, I guess I forgot to tell you. We decided that they don't have to prove it as long as they promise not to make stuff up," Jessie explained.

"Who exactly is this *we* who decided everything?" Marla asked, putting her hands on her hips.

"Nat and I," said Jessie.

"Do I have to remind you *again* that we are supposed to make all our decisions together?" asked Marla.

"Why are you making such a stink?" asked Jessie. "I talked to Nat on the phone yesterday and we decided, okay?"

"No, it's not okay. I expect my best friend to keep

her word," Marla said, her voice shaking a little, like she was about to cry. "You said we were going to be doing this together. If you don't care what I think, then you can just do this by yourself."

Marla stormed off across the schoolyard in a huff. Jessie started to go after her, but Fink stopped her.

"Don't go yet, Jessie," he said. "It's my turn to tell you my fact."

"Okay, but make it fast," she said, looking across the yard to the spot where Marla was standing, tapping her foot in a way that even from far away you could tell she was really mad.

Fink pulled the slip of paper out of his pocket. "Polar bears can smell their prey from eighteen miles away," he said proudly. "Beat that!"

Jessie was watching Marla, who was now kicking her foot in the dirt, raising a little cloud of dust.

"I have to go," she said.

"No, Jessie!" said Fink. "Not until you make your judgment. It should be easy this time. Isn't it obvious which one is better?"

"Yeah, actually it is. I pick the ice cream sundae,"

she said. Then she took off running across the yard toward her friend.

Fink hit the roof. "What is going on here?" he shouted. "This can't be happening!"

"It's just a game, Fink," I said. "It doesn't matter."

"That's easy for you to say — you won again!" said Fink. "You would think it mattered if you were in my shoes."

I bent down and scratched my knee. Fink glared at me. "Don't pull that now. You probably don't even itch. You're just trying to distract me," he said.

"Distract you from what?" I said, standing back up and facing him.

"From figuring out what's really going on here," said Fink. "But guess what. It's too late. I just figured it out. I may be a little slow, but I finally figured it out. She's crooked, isn't she? That's what it is, she's crooked!"

"Who's crooked?" I asked.

"Jessie. She's a crooked judge. You bribed her to vote for your facts," Fink said.

"You're nuts! You think I *bribed* her? With what?"

"I don't know, but she gave it away when she said you two talked on the phone yesterday. You didn't think I'd notice, but I did," Fink said.

"We talked on the phone because she called to say she wanted to make a rule for our game, Fink. That's it."

"Yeah, right. What do you think I am, blind?"

"No. I told you, I think you're nuts," I said. "I can't help it if Jessie voted for my facts. She thought they were more interesting, that's all. Just like she thought *faboo* was better than *bodacious*."

Suddenly, Fink slapped himself in the forehead the way people do when they think they've figured something out.

"Of course! It's the ants! I should have remembered the ants," he said.

I was really starting to wonder if Fink had lost his mind. "What ants?"

"Come on, Nat. I was there, remember? I saw the way you two were with those ants."

"Are you talking about the ants at nature camp?" I asked.

"You know I am."

"What do the ants have to do with anything?"

"You said Jessie would make a good judge because she doesn't like us."

"So? It's true, she doesn't like us," I said.

"Very tricky, Nat-man. She doesn't like *us*, she likes *you*. I can't believe I fell for that!"

"Jessie doesn't like me," I said.

"She hugged you at camp, didn't she?" Fink said. "You told me so yourself."

"She didn't do that because she likes me! She did that because she thought I had saved her from Mad Dog after he stepped on our anthill."

"See? That's what I'm talking about," said Fink, pointing his finger at me. "*Our* anthill! You guys are in this together. You're both cheating!"

It was bad enough that Fink had blamed me for getting him in trouble with Mad Dog the day before, but now he was accusing me of cheating.

"I quit!" I said. "I'm not playing this game anymore. You're being a total bad sport."

"Oh, no you don't! You can't quit while you're ahead," said Fink. "*That's* being a bad sport."

"I only agreed to play because I thought it might cheer you up," I said. "But since that didn't happen, forget it, Fink. I'm not doing it anymore."

I started to walk away, but Fink grabbed me by the arm.

"Wait! Play one more time," said Fink. "That's all I ask. I just want to beat you once, fair and square."

"I don't want to play," I said. "If I win, you'll accuse me of cheating again."

"No, I won't. Because next time, we'll make the facts anonymous. That way, Jessie won't be able to tell whose is whose."

"I don't want to play," I said.

"Just once more? Please, Nat-o? For me?"

"Okay, fine," I finally said.

"Good. Now, we both have to make sure that we type our clues on white paper, so she won't be able to tell from the handwriting," Fink said.

"Okay," I said.

"And we won't fold them this time, so she can't tell by the way the papers are folded whose fact is whose," said Fink.

"Gee, maybe we should wear gloves, too, so she can't dust them for fingerprints," I said sarcastically.

Fink didn't laugh. He was dead serious about all of this.

I looked across the yard and saw Marla and Jessie leaning against the fence, arguing. Jessie pointed over in our direction a couple of times and Marla kept shaking her head. This game sure was causing a lot of trouble. Then, all of a sudden, I saw Jessie throw back her head and laugh. Then Marla laughed, too. So much for the argument. It sure hadn't taken them long to make up.

The bell rang. It was time for us to go back inside. Fink and I started walking toward the building together. I wanted us to make up, too.

"You don't really think I bribed Jessie, do you, Finker?" I asked.

"I don't know," he said. "I just think it's weird that she chose your facts both times, that's all."

"You have to admit, a twenty-four ton ice cream sundae *is* pretty faboo," I said.

"Where'd you find that fact, anyway?" he asked.

I thought about saying the same thing he had said to me earlier about not wanting to reveal my secret sources to the competition, but I decided against it and answered his question instead.

"Mrs. Townsend told me about the sundae," I said. "She was on the hot-fudge committee."

"Mrs. Townsend, my clarinet teacher?" asked Fink.

I nodded.

"You asked *my* clarinet teacher for a fact to out-faboo me?" asked Fink.

"Not exactly," I said. "I didn't ask her for it, she offered it to me."

"Oh, great," said Fink. "Now you've got her on your side, too. It's a conspiracy."

"She's not on my side," I said. "She had an appointment with my mom. My mom talks to all of her patients while she's working on them, so I guess she told her about our game. It's not a conspiracy, Fink, it's just . . . orthodontics."

"Why didn't Mrs. Townsend tell *me* about the sundae?" Fink asked. "After all, I'm the one who's her student."

"Maybe it's because you're *appalling*," I said.

It was supposed to be a joke. Normally, I could say something like that to Fink and he would laugh. But nothing had been normal with Fink lately.

After school that day, Fink and I went to the Bee Hive for a snack. We sat together at a little round picnic table while Fink drank a strawberry froozle and I had a jumbo orange juice with lots of crushed ice.

"I wonder how much ice cream it takes to make a twenty-four ton sundae," I said.

Fink shrugged. "Remember, you have to type your fact tonight. White paper and no folding," he said.

"Can't we talk about something other than the game, Fink?"

"You're the one who brought up the sundae," he pointed out. "If you want to talk about something else, go ahead. I'm not stopping you."

"Okay. Do you want to hear about Tallulah's new trick?" I asked.

"I guess so," he said.

"Too bad, because she doesn't have one," I told him. "I've tried to get her to roll over, but no matter how much cheese I give her, she just won't do it."

Fink reached for a napkin, and when his sleeve pulled up, I noticed a couple of long red scratches on his arm.

"What happened to your arm?" I asked.

"Nothing," he said, quickly pulling his sleeve down to hide the scratches.

"Did Picklepuss do that?" I asked.

Picklepuss is Fink's cat. She's very friendly. I've never seen her scratch anybody. Her breath smells kind of fishy, and sometimes she coughs up these really disgusting hairballs, but other than that, she's a very nice cat. Not at all the kind of cat that would scratch up your arm like that.

"She didn't mean to scratch me," said Fink. "It was my own fault. I was annoying her."

"You've been annoying me lately, and I haven't scratched your arm," I said. Again, I was trying to be funny, but Fink didn't laugh at my joke.

"Look, I've got to get going," he said, standing up and going over to the trash to throw out his cup.

I looked at the seat of Fink's pants. "Uh, Fink? I hate to tell you this, but I think you sat in something gross."

Fink turned around, looked at his pants, and sighed. "Great," he said, touching the sticky pink stain, "it's gum. My mom's going to kill me. She just bought me these pants."

"Maybe I can help you get it out."

"Forget it," he said. "What do you know about getting gum out of pants? Have you ever sat in gum?"

"No," I said.

"Of course not," he said. "People like you don't sit in gum, do they?"

People like me? Yesterday that had meant people who didn't try to figure out why their knees itched. What did it mean this time?

"We're just different, that's all," said Fink.

When Fink and I first became friends all the way back in kindergarten, our moms used to joke about how we were like two little peas in a pod. Sure, we're different in some ways, but in the most important ways — the ways that really matter — Fink and I have always agreed that we're alike. What had happened to suddenly make Fink change his mind about that?

On the way home, I tried to convince Fink to come over and help me teach Tallulah how to roll over, but he turned me down.

"I've got stuff to do," he said.

"What kind of stuff?" I asked, hoping maybe he'd invite me to join him. I felt like we needed to spend some time together. Regular time, away from school and Mad Dog and Jessie and Faboo Facts.

"Just stuff," he said.

I wasn't getting anywhere with him, so I let it drop.

When we got to his house, Fink walked up the steps and started to open the front door. As I stood on the sidewalk watching him, a riddle I'd heard a long time ago popped into my head. *Question: When is a door not a door? Answer: When it's ajar.*

Before he went inside, Fink turned and called, "Hey, Nat?"

Maybe he had changed his mind and decided to invite me over after all.

"Yeah, Fink?" I called back, coming a few hopeful steps closer.

"Remember not to fold your fact."

"Oh," I said. "Okay. I will."

"And wear your baseball hat tomorrow," he told me.

"Why?" I asked, but he had already gone inside and closed the door.

As I started walking the rest of the way home, I found myself thinking about the door riddle again. *When is a door not a door?* But why was I thinking about riddles? Riddles aren't real questions; they're made-up questions with made-up answers that we ask each other just for fun. I didn't have time to be asking made-up questions. Not when I had so many real ones that needed answering. Why was my best friend all of a sudden acting all weird with me and telling me we were so different from each other? And why didn't he want to come over, or hang out with me and Tallulah, or talk to me, or let me help him get gum off his pants? And why did it seem like the only thing he really cared about anymore was beating me at some silly game that wasn't even fun to play?

Question: When is a Fink not a Fink?
Answer: When he's in a funk.

CHAPTER SEVEN

So, I had two things to figure out now. One, why was my knee itching, and two, why was Fink in a funk?

I was getting pretty good at keeping track of warnings from my knee with my Itch Log, so it occurred to me, maybe I should start a Fink Log, too. That way, I could keep track of all the little things that bugged him, and maybe figure out how to get him back to normal. Of course, usually, if one of us was bugged about something, we would have just talked it out together, probably up in our tree. But now I'd noticed that whenever I asked Fink what was bugging him, it seemed to bug him even more.

By the time I'd finished making the Fink Log, I had a pretty long list of things I could remember that had bugged Fink lately, including all the times I asked him what was bugging him. First on the list was the fact that Jessie had chosen the name *Faboo Facts* instead of *Bodacious Facts*. Then there was the fact that I'd won the first two rounds of the game. Maybe the answer was simple — Fink was bugged about the game. But then I remembered how weird he'd been with me after the math test when he'd accused me of bragging, and how he'd hidden the scratches on his arm, and the way he'd acted after he sat on the gum. None of those things had anything to do with the game.

My head was spinning, so I decided to take a break from the logs and work with Tallulah for a while on her trick. I was determined to get her to roll over.

"Come on, girl," I said as I carefully lifted her out. We did our nose thing and then I put her down on my bed and let her sniff a little piece of cheese I'd brought up to my room. "You can do it," I said as I gently tried to push her over. She dug her little claws into the bedspread and refused to let me turn her over. I tried a couple more times and then I gave up. I picked her up and looked into her beautiful pink eyes.

"Why won't you do it?" I asked. "What's the matter, Tallulah? Are you in a funk like Fink? A rat funk?"

The phone rang a couple of times that afternoon, and each time I hoped it would be Fink, but it never was. My mom came upstairs at five o'clock to check on me when she got home.

"Did you teach Tallulah how to roll over yet?" she asked me, looking in at Tallulah, who was happily running in her wheel, her long tail curled up so that it wouldn't get caught in the spokes.

"Not yet," I said.

My mom says she likes Tallulah, but she doesn't ever want to hold her or touch her. She says it would creep her out. I think that's pretty weird, considering that she spends all day putting her fingers in people's mouths, including Mad Dog's! I guess it really is true — one man's trash is another man's treasure.

"Hey, I meant to ask you," my mom said. "How

did you do on that math quiz? The one about the fractions."

"I got a hundred," I told her.

"That's my boy!" she said. Then she kissed the top of my head and went downstairs to make dinner.

I didn't have much homework, so once I'd finished, I got to work looking for a new fact for round three. I still didn't want to play, but Fink had said this would be the last time, so I found a book of world records on my mother's bookshelf and started reading. There was some good stuff in there, including Mrs. Townsend's giant sundae! Looks like I would have been able to prove it without bringing her to school, after all.

After about ten minutes of searching, I finally decided on this — The world record for rocking nonstop in a rocking chair is 480 hours. I started to write it on a slip of paper, but then I remembered what Fink had said about typing it.

The next morning, with my typed, unfolded piece of white paper in my backpack along with my two logs, I walked to the corner to meet Fink. He wasn't there yet, so I waited a few minutes. When he didn't show up, I walked to his house and rang the doorbell.

"Oh, hello, Nat," said Mrs. Fink when she opened the door.

"Is Boyd ready yet?" I asked her.

"Oh, didn't he tell you? He had to go to school early this morning," she told me.

On the way to school, I tried to figure out why Fink could possibly have had to go to school early. I came up empty. I couldn't think of a single reason.

When I got to the yard, he was nowhere in sight.

"Hey, Nat, looking for your friend Fink, by any chance?" Mad Dog asked when he saw me standing around by myself.

"Maybe," I said.

"I can tell you where he is if you want to know," he said, "but it's going to cost you. Got any gum?" he asked.

I shook my head.

"How about mints?" he asked.

"No," I said, "the only thing I've got in my pockets is lint."

"Can I have it?" came a soft voice from behind me. It was Leslie Zebak.

"Wait a second. You want his lint?" Mad Dog asked Leslie.

She nodded. "I've got sort of a collection," she said, smiling and touching the locket she was wearing around her neck.

"Get lost, Leslie," I said. "You can't have my lint. And no more fuzzballs, either."

Leslie started to leave.

"Wait, I might be able to help you out," Mad Dog told her. "I noticed a big wad of fuzz in my belly button the other day. It's probably still there. You want it?"

"No, thanks," said Leslie quickly. "I only collect his."

Mad Dog looked disappointed for a second, but then he grinned. "I can get it off him for you if you want," he said.

I swallowed hard. How was Mad Dog planning to get the lint out of my pockets? I guess he could tell I was nervous.

"Relax, I'm not going to hurt you. I just figured since I've got something you want and you've got something I want, maybe we could make a trade," he said.

"Let me get this straight, Mad Dog. Now *you* want my lint?" I asked.

"Not for myself," he said, jerking a thumb in Leslie's direction. "For her."

"Really?" said Leslie. "You'd do that for me?"

"Not everybody knows this, but I'm actually a nice guy," said Mad Dog. "Unless you cross me. Do that, and I don't care who you are, I'll cream you."

Leslie giggled. "You're so funny, Douglas," she said.

"You think?" said Mad Dog. "Want to hear my belch? You might still be able to smell what I had for breakfast."

Leslie didn't seem too excited about that idea, but she didn't walk away, either.

"Okay, Boyd," Mad Dog said, "fork over the lint for the little lady and I'll tell you where your friend is."

It sounded crazy, but what the heck? I wanted to know why Fink had come to school early, and apparently Mad Dog was willing to tell me for the price of a couple of lint balls. I reached into my pockets.

"Here you go," I said. "Now where's Fink?"

Mad Dog smiled and I noticed a chunk of what looked like scrambled egg stuck in his braces. I guess we didn't have to smell his burp to find out what he'd had for breakfast after all. He handed the lint to Leslie, who giggled and ran away with her treasure.

"Where's Fink?" I asked again.

"He's inside with Mrs. West, getting extra math help," Mad Dog said.

"Fink? No way. Where is he really? Come on, I gave you the lint, Mad Dog. Tell me where he is."

"He's inside getting math help. If you don't believe me, go look in the window and see for yourself."

"Our room is on the second floor. How am I supposed to see in the window?" I asked.

"You could climb that tree," said Mad Dog, pointing over to a tall pine tree growing next to the school building.

I've climbed pine trees before, so I knew what it was like. First of all, the branches are prickly, and then there's also the problem with sap. Once you have that on your fingers, it's murder getting it off. Plus, this tree was really tall and all the low branches had been cut off — probably to keep kids from climbing up.

"You're sure he's in there?" I asked, looking up at the window of our classroom.

"Yep," said Mad Dog, "he's there. You want me to boost you up into the tree?"

"No, thanks. But I don't get it. Why would Fink need math help? He rules at math."

"Well, he didn't rule on that last quiz," said Mad Dog.

"What do you mean? He aced it."

"No, he didn't. He flunked it," Mad Dog said.

"How do you know?"

"Because I flunked, too," said Mad Dog. "That's why Mrs. West made us both come early this morning — for extra help, and to retake the test. I finished faster than old Finky boy. Climb the tree and look in the window. He's still up there sweating bullets over it right now. I swear."

Had Fink really flunked the math test? It sure would explain why he'd acted so weird when I told him I'd aced it.

When the morning bell rang and we went inside, Fink was already in the room sitting at his desk. He didn't even look over at me. He just stared out the window, ignoring me and everyone else in the room. I wanted to go over and ask him if what Mad Dog had told me was true, but there were too many people around to have a private conversation, so I waited to talk to him about it at lunchtime.

But Fink didn't want to talk at lunch. He shoved his sandwich in his mouth, finishing it in a few giant bites, gulped down his milk, and put his jacket on. All he cared about was getting outside to play Faboo.

"You didn't fold the paper, right?" he asked. "And you typed it the way I told you to?"

"Yes," I said. "I did it exactly the way you told me to and I also remembered to wear my hat."

"Good, because this time I'm not putting up with any funny business," he said.

"Why do you care so much about this game, Fink?" I asked.

But he didn't answer. He just grabbed my arm and pulled me outside and over to the bench where Jessie and Marla were waiting. As soon as we got there, Fink grabbed my hat off my head without even asking first and handed it to Marla.

"Hey, what are you doing?" I yelled, trying to grab it back. "That's my lucky hat! It took me hours to get the brim bent just right! You're going to mess it up!"

"Eww, it's disgusting," Marla said, wrinkling up her nose and quickly dropping my hat.

"Hey! Watch it!" I said, reaching out and managing to catch it just before it hit the dirt. "I told you, that's my lucky hat."

"It's not lucky for the people who have to smell it," said Marla, waving a hand in front of her nose.

"Give me the hat, Nat," said Fink, holding out his hand.

"No way. You don't appreciate the time it takes to duck a bill properly like this. What do you want with my hat, anyway?"

"We need it for the game. We have to have something to put the facts in," said Fink.

"Won't that hat make them smell?" asked Jessie.

"My hat doesn't smell," I insisted. "My mom washes it in the dishwasher after every game."

"In the dishwasher? Really?" asked Jessie.

"Yeah, it wrecks them if you put them in the washing machine," I explained. "It gets too wet, or something."

"I'm sure you two would love to stand here and talk about dishwashers and laundry all day, but I've got a game to win here. Come on, let's play," said Fink.

"Nobody touches my hat but me," I said.

"If you're so worried about the hat, you can hold it yourself, okay?" Fink said. "Now the judges have to close their eyes while we put our facts in the hat."

Fink and I both put our typed, unfolded, identical-looking pieces of paper in the hat.

"Okay, open your eyes," Fink said. "Pick one and read it out loud."

Jessie pulled one of the papers out of the hat and read what was written on it. "'In Spain, it is common to put chocolate milk on cereal.'"

Of course, I knew that was Fink's fact, but I didn't say anything. The whole point of all this fuss with the papers and the hat was to make sure the judges didn't know whose fact was whose.

Next Jessie read my fact. "'The world record for rocking nonstop in a rocking chair is 480 hours.'"

"At last! This is finally going to be fair," said Fink. "Which one is more interesting? The chocolate milk or the rocking chair?"

Jessie looked at Marla. "What do you think?" she asked.

"Well, I think it's pretty interesting that people put chocolate milk on cereal," she said. "I've never heard of that before, have you?"

Jessie shook her head.

Fink couldn't help himself. He started to smile,

but then he quickly covered his mouth and pretended to cough. Marla wasn't done yet, though.

"I also think it's pretty interesting that someone could sit in a rocking chair for 480 hours. How many days is that, anyway?"

I started to do the math in my head, but Jessie beat me to it. "Twenty days," she said.

"Wow, that's a long time to rock without stopping," said Marla.

"Yeah, I'll bet they had really sore legs after that," said Jessie.

"Come on," Fink interrupted impatiently. "Which one wins, chocolate milk or rocking chair?"

Marla and Jessie looked at each other. "Rocking chair," they said at exactly the same time.

"You've got to be kidding!" Fink shouted. "Let me see his paper! There must be a clue on there, or something he did tipped you off so that you'd know that fact was his."

Fink grabbed my fact out of Jessie's hand and started carefully examining it, front and back.

"If you want to know the truth," Jessie said, "I did know whose fact was whose."

"I knew it!" Fink said. "You guys cheated!"

"No, we didn't," said Jessie. "The clue was on *your* paper, Fink, not Nat's."

"Mine? What are you talking about?" asked Fink. "I didn't put any clue on mine."

"Yes, you did," said Jessie. "You misspelled *chocolate*. You left out the second O. Everybody knows Nat is a better speller than you, so I knew that one was yours."

"That's still cheating," said Fink. "You knew the rocking chair fact was Nat's, and that's why you voted for it."

"But I didn't see the papers," said Marla, "and I voted for Nat's, too."

"Yeah, but that doesn't matter, because your vote doesn't count. You're just a pretend judge," said Fink.

"What does that mean?" asked Marla.

"It means we only let you *think* you were a judge so that we could get Jessie to do it," said Fink.

Needless to say, Marla was furious. She kicked up

an even bigger cloud of dirt than she had the day before. And when she was done yelling and kicking, she turned to Jessie and said, "If you don't quit with me right now, I'll never speak to you again, Jessie Kornblume, and that's a promise."

And then, because unlike Fink and me, these two best friends were on the same side, they both quit.

In a way, I was relieved. Without judges, we couldn't play the game anymore. And between that and the truth being out about Fink flunking the math test, maybe we could clear the air and get back to the way things were supposed to be with Fink and me.

That's what I was hoping, but it's not what happened. Actually, it's not even close.

CHAPTER EIGHT

After Jessie and Marla quit, they went off to jump rope or do some other girly thing like that, leaving Fink and me alone together at the bench.

"Do you want to talk about it?" I asked.

"About what?" said Fink. "The fact that I got rooked out of winning *again* just because I can't spell?"

"No, about why you're in such a funk," I said.

"I don't even know what a funk is, so how am I supposed to answer that question?" asked Fink.

"A funk is like when you fall off the merry-go-round and then you run out of hot fudge," I said, trying to remember the way Mrs. Townsend had explained it.

"Uh, okay," said Fink, "if you say so. It doesn't really matter, anyway."

"What doesn't matter, Fink? Come on. This is me you're talking to, your best friend, the person you used to tell everything," I said. "Don't you think it matters that things are weird between us? Why won't you tell me what's going on?"

The bell rang and kids started heading back into the school. Lunch hour was over and we had five minutes to get back to class.

"There's nothing to tell," said Fink.

"What about the math test? You could have told me you flunked it," I said. "I would have understood. I might have flunked it myself, if it hadn't been for you."

"You wouldn't have flunked it," Fink said. "Everything would have worked out fine. It always works out fine for you. You're a winner, Nat. You know that."

"Well, so are you," I said. "You told me so yourself just the other day."

"Well, it turns out I was wrong. I'm not a winner. At least not anymore," said Fink. "I've lost it."

"Lost what? Your confidence? Fink, you have twice as much confidence as any other person I've ever known."

"Maybe I used to, but look at me now, Nat! I'm pathetic. I can't do math anymore, I can't play the clarinet, I can't make a basket, I can't win at Faboo Facts, I can't spell, I can't even teach my own cat how to do a trick! How can I possibly be confident with all of this going on?"

"Is that how you got those scratches," I asked, "trying to teach Picklepuss a trick?"

Fink nodded. "Cats are supposed to be smart," he said. "I thought maybe if I could teach her how to roll over before you taught Tallulah how to do it, I might feel better."

No wonder Fink hadn't wanted to help me with Tallulah. Everything we did had turned into a competition.

The warning bell rang. I looked around and saw that we were the only ones left out in the yard.

"Come on, Fink, we can talk about this more later," I said. "We'd better hurry up before Mr. Cappart locks the doors. You know how he is about that."

"You go ahead," he said. "I probably can't run fast anymore, either. I'm telling you, Nat — everything I was ever good at before, I stink at now. I've lost it."

I saw Mr. Cappart come outside and start to pull the doors closed. "Let's go, boys!" he called over to us. "Last chance! Door's closing."

"Come on, Fink," I said.

He still didn't move from the spot where he was standing.

"What's the matter with you?" I yelled. "Look, he's closing the doors. I don't want to get a late slip. Hurry up or we'll be locked out."

"Okay, okay, I'm coming," Fink said, and he started to run with me toward the doors.

"Run, Fink!" I yelled over my shoulder to him as I sped across the yard as fast as I could. "Wait!" I shouted to Mr. Cappart. "Don't close the doors yet! We're coming!"

With a final burst of speed, I raced up the steps,

taking them three at a time, and made it just in time to slip in the door before it clicked shut. Fink, however, didn't make it. He was still outside.

"My friend is out there," I said as I tried to catch my breath. "He's usually a faster runner than me, but he's having kind of a hard time right now. Couldn't you make an exception just this once, and open the doors back up to let him in?"

Mr. Cappart seems like one of those people who doesn't make exceptions very often, but I guess he must have felt sorry for Fink. To my surprise, he agreed to open the doors back up.

But when he did, Fink wasn't out there.

Mr. Cappart leaned his head out the door and looked around the yard. "I don't see him, Nathaniel," he said.

I stuck my head out the door and looked around, too. No Fink.

"Where could he have gone?" I asked. "He was right behind me."

"Boyds of a feather stick together," said Mr. Cappart, then he laughed.

Compared to the jokes Fink and I usually get about having the same name, that one was pretty good, especially if you happen to be a person who uses a lot of expressions. "He probably went around front to the office, to get a late slip," said Mr. Cappart. "Don't worry, I'll track him down."

I hurried down the hall back to class.

"How nice of you to join us, Mr. Boyd," said Mrs. West, raising one eyebrow as I slipped into my seat. "And where, pray tell, is your friend Mr. Fink?"

"I think maybe he's down in the office getting a late pass," I said. "He got locked out."

Mad Dog snickered. "What a loser."

I wanted to say something to defend my friend. But talking back to Mad Dog is like coating yourself with honey and lying down in front of a hungry bear. I reached down and scratched my knee, but I didn't bother to record it in my Itch Log. I was too worried about Fink. Where was he, anyway?

Five minutes later, when Fink still hadn't shown up, Mrs. West used the classroom phone to call down to the office. They told her that Fink hadn't ever come in for a pass.

"Do you have any idea where he is?" Mrs. West asked me. She seemed worried, and so was I.

"I'm not sure," I said.

"Did you two have an argument during lunch?" she asked.

"Not exactly."

"Then what do you suppose the problem is?"

"The problem is he's a loser," said Mad Dog.

Okay, once was hard to take, but twice was impossible. I had to say something this time. "Fink is not a loser," I shouted. "He's a great guy. He's just in a funk, that's all."

Mad dog laughed. "Funky Fink," he said. "Finky Funk. Funkity, funkity, Fink Fink."

The whole class cracked up. All except me and Mrs. West. She picked up the phone and called the office again to ask Mr. Cappart to come take over her class.

"I need to go make a call to see if he's just gone home," she told us.

Mr. Cappart showed up a few minutes later, and Mrs. West left to go make her phone call.

"Please take out a book and do some independent reading until your teacher returns," Mr. Cappart told us.

I happened to have brought that world record book from home, just in case Jessie or Marla had insisted on proof about either the sundae or the rocking chair facts. For fifteen minutes, I read about who had grown the longest fingernails, who had eaten the most hot dogs, had the most babies, hic'd the most hiccups. But I didn't care about any of it. All I wanted to know was where my friend was.

When Mrs. West came back, she came over and quietly asked me to step out into the hall with her.

"Are you sure there's nothing you need to tell me about Boyd?" she asked me. "I promise that whatever you say won't go any farther than right here."

Mrs. West never calls us by our first names. It felt funny hearing her say Fink's name like that.

"He told me he thinks he's lost it," I said.

"Lost what?" she asked.

"His self-confidence, I think."

"How did it happen?" she asked.

"Would you wait here a second, Mrs. West? I have to get something."

A minute later I was back with my Fink Log. "Okay," I said, "I think it started at four o'clock on Monday afternoon, when Jessie chose *faboo* instead of *bodacious*. Then it got worse after his crying-sea-turtles fact lost, and then it got really bad when my rocking chair beat his chocolate milk. To top it all off, he flunked the math test, almost kissed Mad Dog's shoe, sat in gum, and his cat won't roll over."

Mrs. West looked stunned. "I think maybe you need to say that all over again, only much more slowly this time," she said.

I explained everything and showed her the log.

Mrs. West smiled. "It's nice to know you've been paying such close attention in science class, Mr. Boyd."

"Anyway, I've been keeping this log, and it seems like all kinds of things are making Fink feel bad these days," I said. "He's not usually like this. You know how he is. He's always so positive about everything. Nothing bothers him."

"Sounds like he's having a little bout of low self-esteem," said Mrs. West.

I had heard people talk about low self-esteem before, but I didn't know exactly what it was.

"Is low self-esteem serious?"

"It can be," said Mrs. West.

"Is there a cure for it?" I asked.

"There's not a magic pill you can take, if that's what you mean, but there are certainly things you can do to help someone who has low self-esteem feel better."

"Like what?" I asked.

"Like reminding them of what's good and worthwhile about themselves," she said, "in case they've forgotten for some reason."

Adults are always saying stuff like that, which sounds good coming out, but when you really think about it, you have no idea what it means. How was I supposed to remind Fink of what's good about him?

"Did you talk to his mom?" I asked. "Does she know where he is?"

"I wasn't able to reach her. I left her a message," said Mrs. West. "But maybe you can figure out where he might have gone. After all, you know him better than anybody in the world."

I felt a lump rise in my throat. I didn't want to cry in front of Mrs. West, but I felt really bad because I knew that used to be true. I did know Fink better than anybody in the world at one time, but not anymore.

"Are you sure you don't have any idea where he might be?" Mrs. West asked me. "Some special place he might go?"

I thought of the tree in my backyard. Would Fink go there by himself? Maybe.

"Do you think it would be okay if I left school early today and went out to look for him?" I asked.

"I'm afraid not," said Mrs. West. "I'm not allowed to dismiss you without your mother's written permission. I'm sure he'll turn up. Try not to worry."

That was easier said than done. All I could do was

sit there watching the second hand crawl around the clock, wishing it would hurry up and be time to go.

When I finally thought I would go crazy from watching the clock, I turned in my seat and looked out the window instead.

I couldn't believe what I saw! There was Fink, sitting in the pine tree right outside the window.

CHAPTER NINE

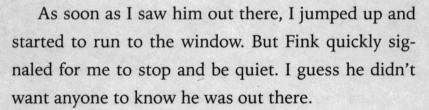

As soon as I saw him out there, I jumped up and started to run to the window. But Fink quickly signaled for me to stop and be quiet. I guess he didn't want anyone to know he was out there.

It wasn't easy, but I did what he told me to do. I went back to my seat and sat there, without telling anybody he was in the tree. I waited for what seemed like hours before the bell rang, then I ran outside to get Fink.

"What are you doing up there?" I called up through the branches.

He giggled.

"It's not funny, Fink," I said. "You scared me. I thought something happened to you."

He giggled again and then I realized, he was laughing because he was scared, too.

"Are you okay, Fink?"

"Yeah, but I'm stuck," he called down to me. "I can't get back down."

There was a big empty cardboard box on the ground under the tree. I guess Fink must have found it and dragged it over there to stand on so he could climb the tree. I hopped up on the box, grabbed a branch, and swung myself up into the branches.

"Ouch!" I yelled as the pine needles poked me.

"Shh! Be quiet! I don't want anybody else to know I'm up here," Fink said.

"Why did you climb up here in the first place?" I asked as I slowly started to make my way up through the branches to where Fink was.

"I didn't want to have to go all the way around to the office to get a late pass, so when Mr. Cappart closed the door, I climbed up the tree. I thought maybe I could get in through the window," he told me.

"You're crazy," I said. "What if Mrs. West had seen you?"

"Fortunately, she didn't," said Fink. "By the way, thanks for standing up to Mad Dog for me like that."

"How did you know?" I asked.

"The window was open," he said. "I heard you."

"It's no big deal," I said. "Come on, take my hand and I'll help you get down."

It was much harder going down than coming up, but together we made our way slowly down through the sappy, prickly branches until we were finally close enough to the ground to jump. Right before we did, though, Fink grabbed my arm.

"Look! It's Mad Dog!" he whispered.

Sure enough, Mad Dog was coming toward us. And he wasn't alone. Leslie Zebak was with him.

"It's just a couple of lint balls," he was saying.

"Well, it was awfully thoughtful of you," said Leslie," and gentlemanly, too."

"Yeah?" said Mad Dog. "Listen, Leslie, can I ask you a question? What do you want with that puny little Boyd kid's lint, anyway?"

"Like I said, I collect it," she told him.

"Yeah, but why?"

"Well, I used to like him," said Leslie. "But actually, to tell you the truth, lately I've been thinking maybe he's not the man of my dreams after all. In fact . . ."

Leslie undid the clasp on the chain around her neck, opened the little locket, and took the lint and fuzz balls out of it. She placed them on her palm, then took a deep breath and blew them away. "I'm through with Nat Boyd forever," she said.

It took all my might not to whoop and holler in celebration at that point, but I didn't. The sun glinted off Mad Dog's braces as he smiled at her, and Leslie Zebak (who was through with me forever!) blinked in the glare, giggling and smiling at her new crush.

I kept my mouth shut until they'd walked far enough away to be out of earshot.

"Hallelujah!" I shouted. "No more stinky love notes for me!"

I jumped out of the tree, and then gave Fink a hand getting down.

"Thanks, Nat-o," he said. "I might have had to stay up there all night if you hadn't rescued me."

"Why didn't you want me to tell anybody when I first saw you up in the tree?" I asked him. "We could have gotten you down sooner."

"I've already been called a wuss and a loser this week," he said. "Just think what people would have said if they'd seen me stuck up in a tree."

"We'd better go inside and tell Mrs. West you're okay, Fink. She was really worried. And you should call your mom, too."

"You don't have to come," Fink said. "I'll take care of it. Just go on home."

"I don't want to go home," I said. "I want to go with you."

"Why?" asked Fink. "Mad Dog was right, you know. I'm a loser, just like that dumb little squirrel the other day. You don't want to have a best friend who's a loser, do you? It'll be bad for your image. Really, you should get going."

"First of all, Fink, since when do you listen to anything Mad Dog says? Second of all, listen to *me*. I know you, and believe me when I tell you, no matter what you think right now, you are *not* a loser. Losers are people who snort when they laugh and make jokes that aren't funny. They pick their noses and don't wash their hair. They like boring movies and bad comic books and they never, ever have good ideas about anything. Losers are people who don't have friends, because they aren't any fun to be around."

"Tell the truth, Nat-o. Have I been any fun to be around lately?" asked Fink.

"No," I said, "but that's not because you're a loser. It's because you're a *sore* loser. I've got it all written down in my log."

"Your Itch Log?" asked Fink.

"No, my Fink Log. I've been keeping track of all the stuff that's been bugging you lately and it all has to do with you losing. Starting with *faboo* beating *bodacious*."

"*Bodacious* should have won," said Fink. "It's a better name. Anybody with half a brain can see that."

"See?" I said. "That's what I'm talking about! You're being a sore loser. Did it ever occur to you that the reason your name lost was because it wasn't as good as the one I thought of?"

"No," said Fink, "that never occurred to me."

"And what about my facts?" I asked. "Did you ever consider the possibility that the reason they got picked was because they were better than yours?"

"No, because mine were better."

"No, they weren't, Fink," I said. "I won because I deserved to win and you deserved to lose."

"You don't understand," he said. "Losing makes me feel like a loser."

"I know. That's because you're so sure of yourself, you hardly ever lose, which is probably why you don't do it very well," I said.

"Losing stinks. Why should I want to do it well?"

"Because if you don't know how to lose well, you could end up really being a loser," I said.

Wow. I even impressed myself when I came up with that. I guess Fink was impressed, too, because for the first time since this whole thing had started, he said something that made sense.

"I guess I *have* been kind of a jerk."

I remembered Mrs. West had said that when somebody had low self-esteem, you were supposed to say nice things to them to help them feel better about themselves.

"You haven't been kind of a jerk, Fink," I said. "You've been a *total* jerk."

It may not have been the nicest thing to say, but at least it was honest. And if you ask me, when it comes to best friends, honesty is the best policy.

"I'm sorry," said Fink.

"It's okay," I said. "Just knock it off already, will you?"

"I'll try, Natalie."

I was so relieved that things were on their way back to normal, I didn't even mind that nickname this time.

We went inside and found Mrs. West. She was glad that Fink was okay, but she was pretty upset about his climbing the tree.

"What on earth possessed you to do such a foolish thing, Mr. Fink?" she asked.

"It wouldn't have been foolish if it had worked,"

said Fink. "And it probably would have, too, if I'd had a little more time and some gloves. I'm sure I could do it."

Like I said, things were on their way back to normal.

Fink called his mom. She had just gotten home from the grocery store and hadn't even checked her messages yet. She wasn't mad — except about the pants. She told him he'd have to pay for a new pair out of his allowance.

"No more froozles for me for a while, I guess," he said sadly as we walked home.

"Well, I do owe you a bunch from the Jinx on Froozles game," I said. "You could make me pay up."

"Nah, that's just a game, Nat. I wouldn't really take your money," he said.

"Want to come over?" I asked when we got to our street. "I could really use some help teaching Tallulah to roll over. Or we could try to teach Picklepuss first, if you'd rather."

"Forget about Picklepuss," said Fink. "Tallulah's much smarter. I'll come help you."

So we spent the afternoon together, trying to get Tallulah to roll over.

"Where there's a will there's a way," I told Fink.

"Yeah," said Fink, "but it helps a lot if you've got some cheese, too."

The next Saturday morning, Fink called early.

"Time me," he said, "I'm coming over."

Fifty-six seconds later, he burst into the room.

"You broke your record!" I shouted.

"Of course I did," said Fink. "My mom got a new box of Crackle Puffs and I had a big bowl of them this morning for breakfast. I told you that was the problem last time; the eggs were slowing me down. Hey, I bet if we give Tallulah some Crackle Puffs instead of that boring old cheese you're always making her eat, she'd roll over like crazy."

"Yeah, but she'd probably also get a mouthful of cavities, like a certain other person I know," I said.

Later that day, Fink and I went down to Miller's Marsh to see if there were any tadpoles around yet.

We brought along a couple of big glass jars with holes punched in the lids and some nets just in case.

"You know, I've been thinking," I said as we waded out into the muddy water with our nets. "Maybe we should give that word game you made up another chance."

"Which word game?" asked Fink.

"You know, the one where you have to say which word is funnier," I said. "Remember, *poodle* or *puddle?*"

"Oh, yeah. Really? You like that one?" he said.

"Yeah," I said.

"You want to play right now?"

"Sure," I said. "You start."

"Okay, which is funnier — *sponge* or *sprinkle?*"

"*Sprinkle,*" I said.

"How about *sprinkle* or *squat?*" he asked.

"I guess *squat,*" I said.

"*Jiggle* or *juggle?*" he asked.

"*Jiggle,*" I said.

"*Droopy* or *flabbergast?*" he asked.

I laughed. "*Flabbergast,*" I said, and laughed again.

"*Funk* or *chunk?*" asked Fink.

"*Funk* isn't funny at all," I said.

"Believe me," said Fink, "I know."

I looked over at my best friend, up to his knees in muddy water, pretzel crumbs all over the front of his shirt from the stash he'd put in his pocket. We were both laughing at this silly game he'd made up for us to play together, and I realized in a flash why my knee had been itching. It had been warning me about the worst thing that could have possibly happened to me — losing Fink's friendship.

"Do you think Leslie Zebak's going to keep Mad Dog's lint in her locket now?" Fink asked.

"She might need something bigger than a locket," I said. "Like maybe a dump truck."

"You don't think she's going to change her mind and like either one of us again, do you?" Fink asked. "That would be awful."

"Don't worry, lightning never strikes twice in the same place," I said.

"Is that just an expression, or is it an actual fact?" asked Fink.

"I'm not sure, but if you want me to prove it, I

could look it up in my record book — or better yet, we could call Jessie and Marla and ask them."

Fink looked horrified.

"Relax, Finker. I was just kidding," I said.

"Uh-oh," said Fink, suddenly pointing behind me. "Look, here comes Leslie. I think she's bringing you another love note!"

I whirled around in a panic.

Fink laughed. "Just kidding, Nat-man. Now we're even."

NAT'S MOM'S CORNY EXPRESSIONS

Do you remember reading these expressions?
Can you finish them? Look back through the book.
When you find the saying, fill in the blank lines.
Jot down the page number, too!

1) Close only _____ in _____.   _____

2) _____ is the mother of _____.   _____

3) The way to a man's _____ is through
   his _____.   _____

4) A _____ and his _____ are soon parted.   _____

5) _____ makes _____.   _____

6) The apple doesn't _____ far from the _____. _____

7) _____ is the best _____.   _____

8) Where there's a _____ there's a _____.   _____

9) _____ never _____ in the same place
twice.   _____

10) One man's _____ is another man's
_____.   _____

ABOUT THE AUTHOR

Sarah Weeks has written numerous picture books and novels, including *Mrs. McNosh Hangs Up Her Wash; Two Eggs, Please; Follow the Moon;* and the popular *Regular Guy* series for middle-grade readers. *My Guy*, the third in that series, is currently in production at Disney for a feature-length, live-action film.

Ms. Weeks is a singer/songwriter as well as an author. Many of her books, such as *Angel Face, Crocodile Smile,* and *Without You,* include CDs of her original songs. She visits many schools and libraries throughout the country every year, speaking at assemblies and serving as author-in-residence. She lives in New York City with her two teenage sons.